Sexy

Sexy

Joyce Carol Oates

HarperTempest
An Imprint of HarperCollins*Publishers*

Sexy

Copyright © 2005 by The Ontario Review, Inc.

All rights reserved. No part of this book may be used or reproduced in any manner whatsoever without written permission except in the case of brief quotations embodied in critical articles and reviews. Printed in the United States of America. For information address HarperCollins Children's Books, a division of HarperCollins Publishers, 1350 Avenue of the Americas, New York NY 10019.

www.harpertempest.com

Library of Congress Cataloging-in-Publication Data
Oates, Joyce Carol, date
    Sexy / Joyce Carol Oates.—1st ed.
        p.   cm.
    Summary: Sixteen-year-old Darren Flynn, a popular, good-looking high school athlete who lacks self-confidence, learns that his jock friends are hatching a revenge act against their English teacher for failing a member of the swim team.
    ISBN 0-06-054149-0 — ISBN 0-06-054150-4 (lib. bdg.)
    [1. Teacher-student relationships—Fiction. 2. High schools—Fiction. 3. Schools—Fiction. 4. Self-confidence—Fiction.] I. Title.
PZ7.O1056Se 2005   2004004402
[Fic]—dc22   CIP
                                                                           AC

Typography by Ali Smith

1 2 3 4 5 6 7 8 9 10

First Edition

For the Darrens

1

Soon as he turned sixteen, put on weight and began to get attention for his looks, things began to turn weird.

Being a swimmer, advanced to the varsity team at the end of his sophomore year at North Falls High, also a promising diver, what Coach called "up-and-coming," he got more attention.

People began to say how good-looking he was. In the street, older girls and even women in their twenties would turn to watch him. Even some teachers, teasing: "Darren Flynn could pass for Brad Pitt's younger brother."

Oh, sure! Darren went red in the face, glowered and turned his lower lip inside out to look as ugly as possible.

To hide his odd silvery-gold hair, he wore a grungy

Red Sox cap reversed on his head. A grungy NFH purple-and-cream sweatshirt frayed at the cuffs. Rotted old salt-stained Nikes on his size-eleven feet.

In a hot mood, his skin erupted at his hairline. And across his upper back, flaring and itching like hives.

Girls liked to say about Darren Flynn that he was sexy, but shy. Or he was shy, but sexy.

Darren was a guy's guy, basically. Unmistakably a jock. Laughing and relaxed with his friends, but with girls this weird kind of light would come into his face as if his mind were struck blank. Like he could see how girls were drawn to him like those sad little moths drawn to the light, beating their wings and crowding one another desperate for the light, and when it's switched off, the little moths are like, *What? What happened? Where is—?*

Darren Flynn would light you up from inside, just the way he looked at you. Make you feel like you were somebody special. Then suddenly he backs off, blushes and mumbles something and walks away and you're standing there blinking as if the light has gone—where?

Thinking, *Next time I won't fall for it. Let Darren try*!

Next time, same damn thing happens.

The way Darren Flynn had of getting inside a girl's head.

2

Inside his head, oh, man, was it strange! He hated it, some days.

Sexy was how he felt, a lot. Like he was charged up and ready to explode.

Hot. Hard-on.

And the word *fuck* intruding into his thoughts like a floating virus he couldn't control. Say he's talking to someone, a girl, a teacher, his own mother, and *fuck* floats in, or some really raw porn-type picture, and Darren goes hot in the face, stammers and mumbles and walks away.

Fuck was a word you heard on cable TV and lots of other places but were forbidden to say at home (at least when Darren's mother might overhear) because it was vulgar, "lowlife" and "trashy." *Fuck suck cock* were similar words Darren and his older brother,

Eddy, were not supposed to say at home. (Their father wasn't so fussy, how his sons spoke. Walt Flynn worked construction for the county; his speech was what you'd call casual.)

"Boys, we are not trailer trash. You will be judged by your language and your manners. Watch your mouths!"

Edith Flynn tried to speak lightly and playfully, but her sons heard the quaver in her voice, almost a kind of fear. Exchanging a glance over her head, Eddy with a shrug, grinning as if to say, *Poor Mom, better humor her*.

Strange to Darren, his mother was so upset by words. She'd been a nurse before marrying Walt Flynn. You'd think a nurse would be experienced and no-nonsense about some things.

Sex, sexy. Sexual. "Man is a sexual being," Darren had read on the Internet, and these words ran through his head, a strange way of thinking, but wasn't it true? In biology class, sophomore year, they'd learned that everything was "reproduction of the species"—"adaptation and survival of the species"—so why did people try to pretend they were ninety-percent spiritual beings? Religious people, most adults in fact, but it was obvious that "Man is a sexual being," wasn't it? Darren wasn't the kind of student who waves his hand in class and asks questions, he wasn't even the kind of student who lingers after class to ask questions, but one day, blushing and stammering, he waited until the others had left the room to ask the teacher, Mrs. Robley, what was the point of it, just reproducing the species, over and over passing on DNA, was that all it was? what did it add up to? and Mrs. Robley looked at him kind of startled, as if Darren Flynn had begun speaking in a foreign language, and smiled and said that was a good question she could answer for him at another time, this wasn't an ideal time, maybe tomorrow, Darren?

Next day, Darren Flynn was one of the first out of the classroom.

His grade in biology was B–. Darren figured it had to be a gift.

Sex, sexy. His mind swerved in this direction, like a badly trained dog straining at the leash. Do you yank the dog back, hard? Do you let the dog drag you?

If he thought too much about these things, he'd get aroused. If he got aroused, his hand might move to grip himself in that special way. He hated losing him*self*, somehow.

He wondered, would it get worse?

3

This year, his junior year at North Falls High, when Darren Flynn's life cracked in two.

Sixteen but sometimes he felt younger. Thirteen, or twelve.

But sometimes he felt older, too. Kind of fed up, burned-out, so many people looking at Darren Flynn in expectation of—what?

Good work, Darren. But you can do better.

Coach Ellroy was always saying this. Darren knew it was a compliment; definitely Coach didn't say this to all the guys. Still, it stuck in his head. As Darren dragged himself out of the pool streaming water, streaming hair down into his face, sucking for air like he'd almost drowned.

. . . can do better.

You can do better.

Hearing these words made Darren blush. Felt a choking sensation he swallowed hard to dislodge.

"OK, Coach. Thanks. I'll try."

Darren wasn't (yet) one of the stars of the team. Coach spoke of him in a "transitional" phase: improving, steadily improving, who knew how far his "potential" would take him? The fastest freestyle swimmer and the most competitive was Jimmy Kovaks, a friend of Darren's who was also a junior, but like so many guys, Jimmy could screw up under pressure.

Practice, practice! Then something happened, anyway.

The most recent meet, against Lebanon High. Lebanon had been the district champs the previous year. Still, North Falls was ahead when Darren dived from the high board, a half gainer; the crowd burst into applause, he'd executed the dive so well, the best he'd ever performed at any competition, yet one of the judges didn't see it that way and scored him lower than a showy Lebanon senior who had a sports scholarship to Ohio University.

There was a jinx, Darren would fuck up. Somehow.

For a diver, it was really scary. Swimming is tense enough, your competition is visible beside you, ahead of you, a desperate situation when your competition is pulling away ahead of you, but diving is worse; up there exposed for everyone to see. Darren climbed up to the high board in a haze of panic, trying to keep his lips from trembling. Trying to look calm, impassive. And there's that silence in the crowd, that expectation. Hundreds of eyes riveted on Darren Flynn in his school-color Speedo trunks.

Won't make it, Dar-ren. Fuckup Dar-ren.

That voice. Jeering, childish. On the JV team he hadn't heard it, but this year he was hearing it, and not only on the diving board—at other times too. Like some part of Darren didn't want him to succeed. Didn't want him to be happy, or make

his father proud of him, didn't want the specta-
tors seated on the bleachers to applaud and cheer.

This voice inside Darren's head, his enemy.

Who?

4

. . . some of them staring at him, eyes fixed and hungry on him, were not girls and young women but men. Seeing in their eyes what they were thinking, and it disgusted him; it scared and excited him knowing his power. Except it was not his power really. Except he did not want it really. Sometimes the men (Darren was disgusted to think this, really grossed out) were adults known to him in town, men who knew his family.

Sex, sexy. Sexual being.

He'd learned to lower his eyes. Never make eye contact.

5

Good work, Darren! But you can do better.

Wanting to twist his lower lip inside out, expose the veiny-wormy flesh in the ugliest gesture he knew.

Except: "Yes, sir."

Or: "Yes, ma'am."

A polite boy. Well-mannered if slightly awkward in confined spaces. Nobody would guess (his mother vowed) the Flynns were not well-to-do, lived out in the country on Route 11 and not in town. Nobody would guess (even more important!) no one on either side of the Flynn family had gone to college.

It was a surprise to Darren, junior year was so much harder than sophomore year had been. Why, he didn't know. Hadn't expected it. Instead of biology taught by a mild-mannered older woman, there was chemistry taught by short, squat, frowning-impatient Mr. Labrador, who scrawled chemical symbols and equations on the blackboard so rapidly, his chalk broke. There was American history, a morass of names, facts, dates, "issues." There was math: "APC Alive" (Applied/Computational). And, Darren's bad luck, English with Mr. Tracy and not Ms. Katzman.

When Darren got swamped with work, feeling like he was drowning, there were lots of friends to offer help. Mostly girls.

Of these, Molly Rawlings was Darren's closest friend. Darren had known Molly since grade school; he'd taken her to dances and parties since eighth grade. A "nice" girl. A "rich" girl. (By North Falls standards.) A virgin, obviously.

Darren didn't want to think that Molly was in love with him, didn't want to think he was (maybe) taking advantage of her, she was always so willing to help him with schoolwork.

It wasn't cheating, exactly. Everyone did it.

In fact Darren Flynn would never *cheat*. Not actually.

His conscience would keep him awake at night if he truly cheated. Copying someone else's work, "plagiarizing." Not that cheating was a big deal in itself, but cheating gave you an unfair advantage over your classmates and friends.

Even Darren's brother, Eddy, who scorned most "beliefs" as bullshit, agreed you never betrayed your friends.

Your guy friends, at least.

A guy's guy. A jock.

Meaning you didn't study, much. You didn't aim for really high grades. You'd go to college (probably, if your parents could afford it), but you weren't obsessing as early as fall of junior year over which college you'd wind up at.

It was cool to get good grades without putting in much effort, but not so cool if in fact you weren't getting the grades, you were falling behind week by week. Darren was having the most trouble with English and history, so much writing, organizing thoughts and arranging "arguments," a part of his brain wanted to shut down in protest.

Life wasn't like that, was it? How much of life needs to be *written*?

That fall, when the thing with Mr. Tracy began. The very beginning. Darren could sit hunched over the keyboard of his clunky old computer working so hard, squeezing his brains so hard, he sweated through his underwear. Had to stop himself from sending e-mail pleas to Molly Rawlings every half hour. *Help!*

Sex was what his mind drifted on to, most. And food. Or food, then sex.

After sex and food, his mind drifted on to sports.

Nothing meant more to Darren than being on the varsity swim team this year. He'd been the star of the JV team, which wasn't saying much, but Coach had "hopes" for him. Coach had told Walt Flynn that Darren had real "promise"—"potential." He'd told Walt Flynn that Darren had about the best attitude he'd encountered in a kid his age.

In the pool, Darren's mind never drifted. On the diving board, never. It was like he climbed up out of his body, so yearning to do well.

Afterward, coming home, collapsing into bed; falling into sleep as if into a deep dark water.

6

School. Classes. Grades.

Not like a team. These are every man for himself.

In high school it was pretty clear that students were being ranked: who was A level, who was OK, who was a loser. It didn't take a rocket scientist to figure this out though teachers tried to be "democratic"—"supportive." Darren's father had gone to North Falls High at a time, he said, when teachers didn't have to care if they were liked or not, and if they disliked you, they didn't try to hide it. If they wrote you off as a loser, they didn't try to hide it.

Darren had begun to realize what he hadn't when he was younger: His teachers were (probably) grading him higher than he deserved because he was a nice kid, and a popular kid, and an athlete, and they felt sorry for him.

Even Mr. Tracy. Sardonic and witty in front of the classroom but surprisingly kind to Darren Flynn, who had such trouble "organizing" his thoughts. Mr. Tracy was encouraging to Darren as you'd encourage a handicapped kid trying out for a team: "Your writing has vigor at first, Darren, then becomes cramped, restrained. As if something clamps down on your imagination and holds you back. As if you're afraid of . . ."

Right. I am.

7

"What the hell's on your mind? Lighten up, bro."

Eddy Flynn had just turned twenty; he'd been out of school for two years and sneered at Darren taking schoolwork and "swim team" so seriously.

Eddy was a careless, likable guy. Always whistling to himself, ready for laughs. At North Falls he'd been a linebacker on the varsity football team but hadn't taken the sport very seriously, missed practices and games and finally got dumped. Nor had he cared about school. To his parents' dismay his grades were low C's and D's, and he'd barely graduated. Eddy sneered at what he called the rich-kid cliques at NFH, who, he said, looked down on guys like him. "Like, we don't live in the ritzy part of town. Dad works for the county and isn't some hot-shit professor or 'dean' at fucking Dartmouth, and Mom used to be a nurse. Like those fuckheads think they're superior to us, and if you think they don't, if you're trying to tell yourself that Darren Flynn is some kind of exception, you're bullshitting yourself, bro."

Bro! This phony black jargon. Darren wanted to punch him.

(You didn't swing on Eddy Flynn, though. Eddy was six feet two and heavier than Darren by maybe thirty pounds. He worked out; his chest was like armor. Built like a fireplug, and under his good-natured demeanor he had a short, hot temper.)

Even more obnoxious was Eddy teasing Darren about Molly Rawlings.

"What's a blow job like, bro, from a Good Girl? I'm curious."

Darren couldn't help blushing. Knew he should play it cool and laugh, but that would be a betrayal of Molly, who was his friend. Every damn time, he let Eddy rile him.

"Go fuck yourself, Eddy."

"Fuck your*self*, bro. I don't need to."

***

Some of these exchanges Edith Flynn overheard.

Saying to Darren he shouldn't let Eddy's teasing upset him.

"Eddy is a little jealous of you, Darren. Try to understand."

"Jealous of *me*? C'mon, Mom."

"He is."

"Why?"

"You know why."

Darren didn't, though. For sure he did not.

8

Gradually it was happening that when he'd had a few beers and was in one of his moods, Darren's dad began to speak vaguely of Darren's going to the U of New Hampshire. Maybe he could major in business, or engineering. There was mechanical engineering, civil engineering. Engineers made good money, and some of them Walt Flynn had met seemed to be nice guys.

(Engineering! As if that were an easy major!)

"Anything's better than working with your hands and back like your old man." Walt Flynn spoke ruefully.

Sure, Darren planned to go to college. Somewhere.

Just hadn't gotten around to thinking about it.

Walt Flynn had had to quit high school at

seventeen to help support his family, after his father had died of a sudden heart attack. First he'd worked at North Falls Textiles, on the Connecticut River, and then, when the mill shut down, like numerous other textile mills in the state, he'd taken what he had thought would be a temporary job with Corinth County: road repair and construction, snow removal, even roadkill patrol.

As a little boy, Darren had begged to accompany his father in the pickup marked CORINTH COUNTY ANIMAL PATROL and help with removing animal carcasses from the roads. Mostly these were white-tailed deer, raccoons, occasionally a foul-smelling skunk. His mother had not wanted him to help with such "grisly" tasks. Ironic now to think that Darren had ever believed such work had a kind of glamour, but when you're a little boy, almost everything your dad does is special.

Later you know better. And your dad knows that you know.

Walt Flynn had been disappointed in his older

son, Eddy, who'd barely graduated from high school and was now hauling gravel for a local stone quarry. "Sure, Eddy thinks he's making 'good money,' but he'll be stuck in that damn nonunion job the rest of his life. If he's lucky, and the stone quarry doesn't go bust."

Looking at Darren with hot, hurt eyes. A look that signaled, *I need to love you better than I love Eddy. Give me the reason.*

In biology class, sophomore year, they'd learned about "natural selection"—"survival of the fittest." Life was like that, you could see: The smartest and strongest got ahead, the dumber and weaker were left behind. Darren hated to think that his father was one of the left behind and thought of himself that way. Darren loved his dad, only just had a really hard time talking with him.

Because all of the talk was *from* Dad to Darren. Dad wouldn't have thought to ask Darren what he was thinking.

All his life Darren had been competing with

Eddy for their dad's attention. Now—it was a strange feeling—Dad seemed to like him better. Or wanted to like him better.

Because I haven't fucked up yet. Not yet.

Plenty of time for that. All of next year, senior year.

Darren's dad tried to get to swim meets when he could, which wasn't often because of his work hours. But each time he'd watched his son swim and dive, he'd been impressed. It didn't seem to matter if Darren wasn't the best. Just he was on the team, and people cheered for him, that was impressive. A while back he'd actually seen Darren win a close two-hundred-meter freestyle race in a meet against North Falls' old rival, Pomfret, and since then he had the conviction that Darren might be awarded a sports scholarship from the U of New Hampshire. Darren knew this was a long shot: His swim times weren't outstanding even for the district, nor was he a star diver even on the North Falls team, which hadn't won a championship in seven years, but it was impossible to explain this to Walt Flynn, who only heard what he wanted to hear. "You got plenty of time to improve, Darren. All next year. Scouts won't be out looking till next year." Also, Darren's dad had been reading about "work scholarships" for students who needed financial aid in New Hampshire.

Darren had read about this too. He'd read that the state legislature was cutting back the university budget for work scholarships.

Try telling that to Dad, though. That stubborn bulldog look to Walt Flynn's face.

". . . just don't want you to throw away your chances, Darren. You can do a hell of a lot better than your brother and your old man, only just you've got to be more optimistic."

Maybe I don't want to do better than you and Eddy, so fuck it!

Aloud, Darren said, "Yes, sir." And blood rushed hotly into his face as if he knew Walt Flynn could read his secret thoughts.

9

Looking at me like he's seeing somebody else, not me. A different son. Somebody who's smarter, a better athlete. Somebody who won't disappoint him.

10

It was in November, a Thursday after swim practice. The thing with Mr. Tracy, Darren's English teacher.

The *thing* was how Darren would think of it, afterward.

The thing that was vague and not-named.

The thing that hadn't happened, anyway.

(Had it?)

At practice Coach had been "disgusted" with several members of the team and especially Darren's friend Kevin Pyne, who'd practically belly flopped his dives and afterward smirked to save face as if he hadn't been seriously trying, which provoked Coach into a withering remark about transferring Pyne to the girls' team, which made all the guys laugh, nothing like hearing somebody else get chewed over by Coach to make you laugh, including even Darren, so Kevin got pissed, his pouty baby face mottled with indignation, he cut out of practice early, and when Darren went looking for him later, his locker was shut and he was nowhere in sight.

"Where the hell's Kevin? He said he'd give me a ride home."

Darren hid the hurt he felt, and the surprise. He'd long ago learned it was better to sound pissed off than to show your true feelings.

The other guys seemed to think that Kevin had split. Watching Darren to see how he'd take it, being dumped by his buddy.

Kevin had his own car now that he was seventeen and old enough for a driver's license. A good-looking Saab only a few years old his father (a vascular surgeon with a practice in Hanover) had passed on to Kevin as casually, Darren thought, as Walt Flynn might pass on to Darren a pair of boots or gloves that weren't the right fit.

Was Darren jealous? No, Darren was not! Only

he had to admit, he liked hanging out with guys like Kevin Pyne and others in their circle, "rich-boy punks," Eddy called them, but fuck Eddy, he was jealous.

Darren finished dressing and left the locker room before anybody else could offer him a ride. He didn't want anybody's charity!

Practice hadn't gone so well for him, either. His freestyle was off and his backstroke he'd been working on wasn't so hot, his dives were barely OK, Coach had only just nodded at him. And he'd gotten a C– on a chemistry quiz earlier. Had to shrug like he didn't really care, hey, it was cool.

This thing that would happen to him, he'd blame on Kevin.

It wasn't the first time that Kevin had let him down. And when Darren saw Kevin next morning in school, Kevin would behave like nothing had happened. The guy never apologized, might mumble, "Something came up, I got a call," so insincere you wanted to laugh in his face, but at lunch he'd be nice to Darren in a flattering kind of way that was hard to resist. You had to accept Kevin on his own terms or not be his friend.

"Is that Darren Flynn? Looking like he needs a ride somewhere?"

Darren was at his locker in the sophomore corridor, shoving his arms into the sleeves of his waterproof jacket, when he heard this airy voice floating toward him like a movie voice. Glanced around to see his English teacher, Mr. Tracy, briskly descending the stairs from the second floor, wrapping a red knit muffler around his neck.

Darren had decided to walk home. It was a mile and a half and starting to snow, but he almost liked it, the sky had turned so dark and the wind had picked up. Sure, he could call Eddy on his cell phone and ask if he'd pick him up after work, except he knew how Eddy would tease him about his rich-boy punk friends, and Darren couldn't deal with that right now.

"Hey, I'm OK, Mr. Tracy. Thanks."

Darren zipped up his jacket. It was a swim-team jacket with a hood: purple with cream-colored letters *NFH*. The fabric wasn't warm enough for November, for a hike home, but at least the jacket had a hood.

"You're sure, Darren? It's no trouble for me."

Outside classes, Mr. Tracy addressed students in a formal, bemused way as if they were actors together in some comedy and he were the one with the script.

Darren mumbled a vague reply. Swung his backpack onto his shoulders. Searched for his gloves. (Shit! Couldn't find them.) Wishing Mr. Tracy would take the hint and leave.

"Were you at swim practice, Darren? How's it going?"

"How's it going?" sounded weird in Mr. Tracy's mouth. Like he was trying to speak some foreign language where he'd gotten the words right but not the inflections.

Darren mumbled what sounded like "OK."

Mr. Tracy was one of the few teachers at North Falls High who supported the teams. He attended basketball games and swim meets and was an enthusiastic supporter of the girls' field hockey team. He'd been at North Falls for only three years and had quickly acquired a reputation for being both well liked and demanding. Darren wasn't one to estimate any adult's age, but he'd have guessed that Mr. Tracy was in his mid-thirties. Not young, but not old. He had a boyish face creased and puckered at the edges, a small ginger-colored goatee and receding hair that lifted in wiry tufts. He wore preppy shirts and pullover sweaters like an aging college student. His eyes were watery and intense behind designer steel-rim glasses. He was about five feet nine, a small-bodied man who paced restlessly at the front of the classroom as he taught, plucking at his beard and breathing through his mouth. Darren appreciated Mr. Tracy's sense of humor. It was rare that a teacher made you actually laugh aloud. And the man was smart, obviously. If you were a serious student having trouble, and willing to work, Mr. Tracy was sympathetic.

Some of the smarter girls, including Molly Rawlings, spoke of Mr. Tracy as "inspirational"—"awesome." It was known that Mr. Tracy had published poetry in *The New Yorker,* but no one seemed to have read it.

Mr. Tracy fell into step beside Darren on their way out of the building. He was talking in his bright, bemused way about one or another school issue, in which Darren hadn't much interest; then, outside, Darren saw with a sinking heart how bad the weather had turned, wet snow swirling out of the dark November sky, and knew he'd better accept a ride home.

From the first, Darren was feeling uncomfortable.

For why did Mr. Tracy turn east out of the parking lot onto Edgewater Street and only then think to ask where Darren lived? in which direction? though already he was headed in the right direction.

Later Darren would think, astonished, *He knew! Knew where I live.*

Another strange thing: Mr. Tracy fussed with the dashboard as he drove. Heat, vents, radio. Telling Darren please buckle up, the roads will be icy, if Darren's "long legs" are cramped, he can adjust the seat. Asking was it warm enough? Too warm? Apologizing for dog hairs. Darren kept mumbling, "OK, Mr. Tracy, I'm fine," and Mr. Tracy crinkled his forehead, asking, "Are you sure?" giving him a serious sidelong look. Weird that any adult would take him so seriously, Darren was thinking. Especially Mr. Tracy with his formal, cultivated ways.

The car was a compact Toyota smelling of something sweetish: not food, more like cologne, hair oil.

Darren was thinking he'd be home in ten minutes minimum. And it really was nice of Mr. Tracy to drive him.

It was so—Darren's long legs were cramped.

Beside Darren, Mr. Tracy seemed very close. He wore a camel's hair car coat and the fleecy red muffler around his neck, and he was breathing through his mouth as he talked, as if he'd been running. He drove with exaggerated slowness like an old-lady driver as gritty snow was blown against the windshield.

"This wind! I'll never get used to it. I've always lived in cities, and life here is so *rural* . . . Were you born here, Darren? In North Falls?"

Darren murmured yes.

"And all your family, I suppose? In this area?"

Darren murmured yes.

"They say North Falls has changed in recent years. New houses, new developments along the river. New residents commuting to Hanover. The school population has gone up. . . . Do you like North Falls High, Darren?"

What a question! As if Darren could compare his school to any other.

"Sure. I guess."

"You're a very popular boy, I've heard."

Darren shrugged, staring out the window. A dull red flush rose into his face.

". . . in our class, and elsewhere. I'm a friend of Mike Ellroy's, and he has told me . . ."

In class, Mr. Tracy had a way of making precise little speeches studded with fancy vocabulary words, but now, driving his car, he was speaking in an almost halting way, breathless as somebody's mother in the eager-to-please mode.

"I've seen you dive. Very impressive. I thought, at that last meet, against Lebanon, the judges were unfair not to rank you higher."

Darren swallowed hard. This was the last thing he wanted to discuss with his English teacher!

". . . wouldn't suppose so, now. But I used to be a swimmer too. Even a novice diver. Not that I could 'compete'—I don't have the physical equipment, as it's called. Tall, lean-hipped, with broad shoulders. An inverted V! In the water, you boys are fast and graceful as torpedo fish. Very impressive."

Darren started out the window, embarrassed.

Thinking how, if the other guys heard this, they'd howl with laughter.

Mr. Tracy went on to ask questions about competitive swimming and diving that revealed he didn't know much about the sport. Thinking that swimmers were born with swimmers' bodies, and not the other way around—they acquired swimmers' bodies through swimming. Darren was uncomfortable with the praise but felt flattered, too. No other teacher at North Falls had said to him the things Mr. Tracy was saying; it was maybe encouraging. Darren had not known that Mr. Tracy was a friend of Coach Ellroy's.

Later he would wonder where his mind had been. Only he wasn't a suspicious person. He wasn't one to think too much about the motives of others when he could barely figure out his own.

Mr. Tracy, driving on South Main, said suddenly, as if he'd just thought of it, "I think I'll stop at the Coffee Cowboy, Darren. Want to come in with me?"

No. Darren did not.

"Want me to bring you anything? Your blood-sugar level must be low, this bleak time of day."

No. Thanks.

In fact, Darren was starving. If he'd gotten a ride with Kevin, they'd have stopped somewhere for sure. But he was reluctant to tell Mr. Tracy this.

Mr. Tracy managed to park close by the Coffee Cowboy and spoke apologetically to Darren, promising he'd be just a minute. "We'll keep the motor running. I trust you, Darren, not to drive off with the car!"

Darren laughed. This was meant to be funny?

The Coffee Cowboy was a popular local place, though Darren never went there. He had no taste for coffee, especially not exotic flavors. You wouldn't think of Mr. Tracy going in the Coffee Cowboy either.

Maybe it was hard to think of Mr. Tracy going anywhere! He wasn't exactly a hot topic of conversation or anybody you'd be curious about, the way the guys were always wondering about Coach Ellroy, what Coach really meant when he said the things he did. For sure, Mr. Tracy wasn't in that category. Girls were more likely to care about him, to admire his "artistic" neckties and laugh at his so-called witticisms, linger after class eager to please him in that way that seems to come naturally to girls. Even a girl like Molly Rawlings.

Molly! Darren remembered he'd been supposed to call her. Damn, he had totally forgotten.

It seemed he was always hurting Molly's feelings. She'd look at him with brimming brown eyes, like she was seeing someone else in Darren's place, someone he was not and did not wish to be. That old song of Bob Dylan's "It Ain't Me, Babe."

Darren was feeling restless, kind of trapped. Wished he'd walked home after all. Almost, he'd have liked to leave before Mr. Tracy returned. Except he couldn't; Mr. Tracy would drive after him, insisting he get back in.

Maybe he'd tell the guys tomorrow about this

ride home. Or maybe not. Anything you told them had to be funny, and would get funnier and cruder in the telling, and actually Darren liked Mr. Tracy, and respected him, and didn't want to ridicule him in public.

Maybe Mr. Tracy was lonely, why he talked so much? So sort of nervous, fluttery? Like Darren's mother when she was in one of her moods talking to a woman friend on the phone, or Darren's father when he'd been drinking (only beer; that was Walt Flynn's weakness) and in that mood that made Darren edgy, Worry About the Future. The worst of it was, with Mr. Tracy and Darren's father they were behaving like you were an adult! They confided in you, things you didn't want to hear, and wanted something from you in return. No way.

There came Mr. Tracy out of the Coffee Cowboy, hurrying. He had not stayed inside long. He was carrying a bag containing not only a tall steaming cup of hazelnut coffee but a bottle of grape Snapple and a large cinnamon twist for

Darren. "I couldn't possibly indulge myself without bringing you something too."

Couldn't resist. Darren's mouth watered so hard it hurt.

"Thanks, Mr. Tracy. It's real nice of you."

"The least I can do. You are a buoyant and helpful presence in our class of sometimes less than scintillating individuals, and as an athlete, you help to make North Falls proud. Enjoy."

Enjoy. There was something about this word, the nudge in the ribs it implied, Darren didn't like.

But he laughed. Mr. Tracy had uttered his little speech in a bright, blithe way like something on TV, funny because it was so corny.

The snow was coming down harder, blown more fiercely by the wind. It must have been just freezing; some of the snow was sleet and struck the car's windshield like tiny metal particles. Mr. Tracy drove with extreme caution through the small North Falls downtown of two or three blocks, holding his coffee cup in his left hand awkwardly and steering with his right. Darren was eating and drinking hungrily, paying only minimal attention to Mr. Tracy's conversation, which continued in that bright, blithe way. Some teachers felt they had to talk like this outside class, maybe. Which was why you tried to avoid them.

The thought came to Darren, he should ask Mr. Tracy for help on the next English assignment. This was a five-hundred-word "spontaneous response" to the essay "Civil Disobedience" by Henry David Thoreau. You were not to consult the Internet or any other source, just write your own thoughts. Darren had tried several times to read the essay, but his mind drifted off; the experience was like hacking through underbrush with a paring knife. Sure it was Great Literature and Profound Ideas, but who cared?

Darren's grades in English this term hadn't been bad so far. It was his first experience with Mr. Tracy, feared by everybody. To his surprise Darren had gotten B's and one C+ and the teacher's lavishly scrawled "Promising!" Not bad for a guy who'd been about the last to learn to read in his first-grade class.

Five hundred words on Thoreau, due Friday morning. Which was tomorrow morning. Darren hadn't even begun. But he was too shy, or too reserved, to ask his teacher about the assignment; also, it wouldn't be fair to the other students.

". . . get along well with your parents, Darren? You seem so well-adjusted."

Darren shrugged, sure.

"A close-knit family, are you?"

Close-knit! Sounded like some kind of sweater.

"Sometimes there's pressure on students your age even their parents don't realize. There can be stress."

Stress. You said it.

The Toyota had made its slow, cautious way through town and was turning now onto Route 11. More sleet, and the windshield wipers sticking. Darren saw that they were drifting toward the yellow line and said sharply, "Watch out, Mr. Tracy—"

and Mr. Tracy immediately straightened the wheel with a little yelp of surprise.

"Sorry, Darren! Driving like this is—well, hypnotic."

Now, on the highway, the speed limit was officially sixty miles an hour, and Mr. Tracy was creeping along at about twenty-five. Other vehicles swung out to pass. Heavy-duty trucks scattered spray across the hood and windshield of the compact car, so Mr. Tracy had to drive even slower.

". . . unlike some of your classmates, you know. The close-knit family is almost a thing of the past. As many as fifty percent of marriages now end in divorce in America! Astonishing. It's never easy, they say, even when divorce has become . . ."

Darren finished the last of the cinnamon twist, washed it down with the remains of the Snapple. He'd been ravenous with hunger a few minutes before but was now feeling mildly nauseated.

". . . hope I haven't been overly inquisitive, Darren. But you are an unusual young person. I don't mean your looks—you hear enough of that, I suppose. Frankly, I'm not one to value others for their looks. It's that you carry yourself with a natural sort of dignity. You're unusually mature for your age. Mike Ellroy remarked you have 'integrity' as an athlete. You 'swim your heart out.' I wish that in our class, you would 'write your heart out.' You seem always to be holding back, Darren. I wonder why."

The hot-air vent was blowing into Darren's face, making him uncomfortable. His body felt too big and clumsy for the compact seat. He was stunned hearing these extravagant words. And Coach Ellroy praising him.

He'd have liked to think this was true. Or true in some way. He was the kid on any team who'd play his heart out, but maybe that was kind of pathetic, too? Wanting so badly to be liked, to belong. Wanting the guys to think he was one of them.

"Yes, Darren? I'm wondering *why*."

Why what? Darren hadn't been following this.

". . . your writing? In my class? You always

seem to be holding back."

"Yeah. I guess."

"Holding back what, do you think? Are there subjects that inhibit you?"

Inhibit. Darren knew what that meant. But it seemed strange, applied to him.

"Maybe you have a talent for drama? Performance? Often—you'd be surprised, Darren—the shyest students become the most uninhibited performers. Do you play a musical instrument?"

"Guess not." Darren mumbled, uneasy. He hated to be, like, interrogated!

Guitar was the instrument he'd play, if he could. His uncle Harvey, his dad's older brother, had actually given Darren one of his acoustic guitars, and tried to teach him to play, last time they'd visited him up in Maine. Darren had been enthusiastic for a while but, back in North Falls, hadn't followed through; lessons were sort of expensive and practicing took time, and one day Mom took the guitar away to store in the attic. But sometimes in his sleep Darren played the instrument as if he knew how—pressing down strings with his fingers, strumming and picking chords the way his uncle Harvey did, like it was no great effort—and a feeling of warmth and happiness spread through him. . . . But when he wakened, it was gone. Like a flame blown out.

"Darren? I hope I'm not embarrassing you? I'm only speaking the truth."

What truth? What were they talking about? Darren shifted restlessly in his seat.

They were passing familiar landmarks made unfamiliar through the wildly swirling snow. North Falls Mobile Home Village, Sunoco gas station and car wash, 7-Eleven, open fields and former farmland and that ugly sign FOR SALE COMMERCIAL ZONING 30 ACRES. A quarter mile ahead on the left-hand side of the highway was the Flynns' house, set back from the road in a two-acre lot. Darren lifted his hand to point it out: "Mr. Tracy, my house is—"

With a sudden rush of emotion, Mr. Tracy said, "'Mr. Tracy'! You could call me Lowell, Darren. That's my name."

In that instant, Darren went rigid. Staring straight ahead through the steamy windshield, shocked as if the man had reached over in a quick agile gesture and touched him.

"—I mean, Darren"—Mr. Tracy awkwardly amended his words—"only that 'Mr. Tracy' is so formal. So archaic somehow, antique . . ."

Darren's face was suffused with heat. His thoughts were confused and furious. What an asshole he was! Getting into this car with Mr. Tracy.

Realizing now, in a rush of guilty knowledge, what he hadn't wanted to remember: that one of the men who seemed always to be staring at him, at swim meets, taking photos of him as he dived, was his English teacher, Mr. Tracy.

"You can let me out here, Mr. Tracy. Right here."

"No, no! Certainly I will take you up to your house, Darren. In this weather . . ."

Rattled, Mr. Tracy braked the car, skidding. He turned too sharply into the other lane, without signaling. There came an immediate angry truck horn from the rear and that sickening hog squeal of hydraulic brakes. Darren steeled himself for a cataclysmic crash, but by some miracle the Toyota skidded across the icy highway and into the Flynns' driveway, and safety.

Before Mr. Tracy could bring his car to a full, shuddering stop behind Walt Flynn's pickup, Darren was out the door with his backpack. Had to escape! Might've muttered, "Thanks!" through gritted teeth; he wouldn't remember afterward. Nor would he remember what Mr. Tracy, anxious words muffled by the wind, called after him.

"Darren? I was sick with worry, wondering where—"

"I had swim practice, Mom. I told you."

"But—this late? It's going on six P.M. And the weather!"

"Me and Kevin stopped for something, Mom. No big deal."

Me and Kevin. Sounded like some ten-year-old kid, calling back over his shoulder to Mom on his way galloping upstairs.

He had to avoid her in the kitchen. One look at Darren's stunned face and she would know.

11

Know what? There was nothing.
It never happened.
I don't have to think about it.

12

He brushed his teeth hard. Really hard.

He rinsed his mouth to get rid of the repulsive sweet-doughy taste.

He would never eat a cinnamon twist again; the thought made him nauseated.

Wishing he could puke up what he'd eaten. Like some girls at school were said to do. Gorging on pizza, ice cream, chocolate cream doughnuts, cinnamon twists and then sticking a finger down their throats, vomiting it all up so nobody would guess what pigs they were in their souls, how repulsive.

Don't have to think about it.

13

Next morning the sky glared with light. And everywhere you looked was a glaze of icy-crusted snow.

So blinding, Darren Flynn wore sunglasses.

"Hey, Flynn, lookin' cool!"

Girls gazed after him, smiling. For basically a shy boy, Darren had a certain sexy swagger.

14

Wanting to cut Tracy's class, but he did not. Wanting never to see that man's face again (watery eyes, spade-shaped gingery beard) in his life, but he would. In English class wanting to slump in his desk, folding his arms tight across his chest in a posture of sullen defiance, but he did not; Darren Flynn behaved pretty much as usual in school that day. Except for the dark glasses.

For that was Darren's way: dignity, integrity. Maturity.

Phony as hell.

Not raising his eyes to Tracy's face, though. Not once in fifty minutes. Not laughing, not even smiling at Tracy's witticisms. (They sounded forced and nervous today, weren't very funny. Only Tracy's cadre of admirers, the Good Girls, laughed appreciatively.)

"Class, may I have your 'spontaneous responses'? I hope the assignment was stimulating, and I look forward to reading a masterpiece or two over the weekend."

Titters, a ripple of dread.

Darren handed in a paper with the others. Maybe it wasn't five hundred words exactly, but almost. He had tried. He was a boy who tried. Fury in his heart, hatred and contempt, yet he tried. Finally printing out his paper at three twenty that morning in a haze of exhaustion and disgust.

"Thank you, thank you. Thank *you*."

The bell rang. Darren Flynn was the first out the door.

15

It was OK with Kevin. You could see he was repentant, sort of. Shoving a chair out for Darren Flynn to sit, in the cafeteria at the guys' usual table by the windows. "Hey, Flynn, what's with the dark glasses? Some kind of celebrity?"

Kevin pronounced the word *say-lreb-ritty*.

Kevin Pyne. Ross Slaugh. Jimmy Kovaks. Roger Polidari.

Darren's buddies. His tight circle. He could count on them.

16

Didn't have to think of it; no one knew.

This thing between him and Mr. Tracy.

This thing that had not happened.

(Had it?)

No one knew, and nothing had happened.

Nothing had happened. That was a fact.

It was a fact! If there'd been witnesses observing him in Mr. Tracy's car . . .

"All he said was 'Call me Lowell.'"

"No, he didn't touch me."

". . . didn't come close to touching me."

"If he had . . ."

I'd kill him.

17

When Darren had been twelve years old, which was almost too old, his father had had a Serious Talk About Sex with him. Oh, man!

This had been a time, in seventh grade, when Darren's body seemed to be changing overnight. From TV and movies he'd picked up certain anatomical facts about females and males both. Of course he'd already been told plenty by Eddy and other guys. By the time the Sex Talk came, Darren knew almost everything Dad would tell him, and some things he would not. Eddy had warned Darren how awful it was: nothing more embarrassing than hearing your father say, "When I was your age," which is the last thing anyone wants to hear from either parent, ever.

Eddy shuddered. "If Dad had said, like, 'jacking

off,' that's bad enough. But Dad trying to twist his mouth around 'mastur-bay-shun'—oh, man!"

Darren had been stricken with embarrassment too. Wanting to tell his father that that was why there was sex education class at school: to spare having to hear your parents say such things.

But Dad's Sex Talk with Darren had been more complicated than his Sex Talk with Eddy had been. For, with Darren, Dad had continued to speak, in a halting voice, about "homosexuals."

News of the sex-abuse scandals in the Catholic Church had been spreading at this time. On TV, in papers. Even Darren, who hadn't been much interested in the news, knew about it. A priest across the river in Norwich had been named as a "serial abuser." And there was a notorious priest in Boston who'd abused hundreds of boys and had been protected by his superiors. Darren had to figure that his father had been influenced by these news items. He had not wanted to think that there might be other reasons.

"Anybody ever says anything to you, Darren, or,

for God's sake, touches you, like in a bathroom, or wherever, you get away from them immediately, OK? I mean, a man or an older kid, could be any age, I guess . . . Not that they're going to kidnap or murder you, but . . . Well, they might. Anyway, you know what I'm getting at, Darren? Gays—homosexuals? People call them fags, but that's kind of a dirty word now. Used to call them queers. Today, people are more what's called politically correct. Meaning . . ."

Darren listened in numbed silence. Nowhere to look except at the floor.

". . . Eddy I never much worried about. He's the kind of boy who can take care of himself. Nobody is going to mess with Eddy Flynn! But you . . ."

Darren chewed at his lip, miserable. He could not believe what he was hearing!

". . . a face like yours, and how kind of quiet, and trusting, you are. Let's just say you take after your mother more than your old man or brother, see. Not that you're the least feminite—femin*ate*?—you are not." Darren's father was laughing nervously, wiping his palms on his burly thighs. He had the air of a man who didn't know what he was saying, only that there was an urgent need to say it, and get it said. His breath smelled of beery fumes.

Walt Flynn went on to say in his halting way that Darren should not get him wrong: He understood that there were laws protecting these people. And lesbians too. He understood that there was a need for such laws. "Like there is a need for laws to protect kids against pedophiles. Like these priests we keep hearing about. See, I'm not against the gay culture. I realize that many of these individuals are good, decent people. They're born with some kind of chromosome or hormone screwup; they can't help what they are. Some of them have operations to switch to another sex, but that's extreme. I got no feelings against them as long as they keep their hands to themselves and off my sons. A gay minister in some church like the Episcopal, that's OK with me. They have women ministers, why not gays? Anybody who comes clean and identifies himself, it's OK with me. But gays pretending to be straight, cruising the mall, video arcades, the Internet . . . Hiding in bathrooms . . . That makes me sick, and lots of other people too."

Darren's father had so worked himself up, he seemed almost to be talking to himself, vague and angry and rambling. Too young to understand that his father wanted to protect him from whatever harm he could, Darren had been stricken with embarrassment and had not known what to say. Wanting to run out of the room. Wanting to erupt into loud, jeering laughter.

Wanting to say he knew what queers were. He knew what fags were. He knew what "gay-boys" were. He knew from Eddy and other, older boys how to deal with them.

"Uh, well, Darren—what d'you say?"

Darren shrugged. Still, he could not meet his father's eye.

"Has anybody ever . . . y'know . . . tried to touch you? Come on to you? Acted funny with you? You can tell me, Darren. You can tell your father."

"I guess not, Dad."

"What d'you mean, you guess not? Don't you know?" Dad spoke excitedly, in a kind of dread.

Quickly Darren said, "Nobody has, Dad. Not ever."

Not ever. This was the only answer Walt Flynn wanted to hear.

Darren's father exhaled, relieved. He'd been sitting heavily on the edge of Darren's bed, and in his wake the corduroy bedspread was damp and twisted.

On his way out of Darren's room, his father reached out to tousle Darren's hair, as he'd done when Darren was a little boy.

Darren had learned not to wince at this gesture, only just laugh. And Dad would laugh too. It was a good feeling.

18

In the steamy bathroom mirror avoiding his eyes. Whoever it was in that mirror.

Face like yours. Not like your brother or your old man. Trusting. Feminite. Feminate?

Looks. Broad shoulders. Lean hipped. Torpedo fish.

Shamed eyes. Guilty eyes. Scared eyes. Eyes to avoid.

Dragging a razor over his stubbled, carelessly lathered jaws, half hoping he'd skin himself.

Oh, Darren! his mother would cry. What on earth have you done to your face!

No school for Darren Flynn today. He's skinned off half his face.

19

A few days later, in Mr. Tracy's fifth-period English class.

It was Mr. Tracy's custom to ask students to read "exemplary"—"outstanding"—papers aloud. Discussion was lively afterward.

This day most of the class participated. Everyone had an opinion about Henry David Thoreau. Except Darren Flynn, who sat impassive, drawing tight little zigzag fishhooks on the cover of his notebook.

Darren wasn't wearing his dark glasses any longer. Still his eyes were lowered, unseeing.

Thoreau's "Civil Disobedience" was the subject. Mr. Tracy paced about excitedly at the front of the room, for he was one to admire Henry David Thoreau. The Abolitionist. The Rebel. The Individual. The Poet. In an uplifted dramatic voice Mr. Tracy read:

"Unjust laws exist: shall we be content to obey them, or shall we endeavor to amend them, and obey them until we have succeeded, or shall we transgress them at once?"

A little shiver seemed to run through Mr. Tracy as he uttered the word *transgress*.

He had a bad cold, though: His eyes were watering; his nostrils looked inflamed. Several times he had to cease speaking and blow his nose into a tissue.

"Excuse me! Hideous cold."

Only Darren Flynn might have noticed: Mr. Tracy plucked at his beard more often lately. He was more rattled, losing his way in one of his show-offy sentences. Pushing his glasses against his nose as they slid down.

Darren thought: *He doesn't know. If I have told anyone. But why would I tell anyone? There was nothing.*

"Darren? Please see me after class."

With his usual flourishes and witty asides, Mr. Tracy had passed back all the papers except Darren's.

Darren knew he'd done poorly on the assignment. What he'd finally printed out in the middle of the night wasn't worth more than a D–; he'd handed it in without rereading it.

The bell rang. As the classroom emptied, Darren shrugged into his backpack and walked very slowly to the front of the room. He'd been taken by surprise, and he didn't like it. Five days had passed since the ride in Mr. Tracy's car, and he'd been feeling better about it, not thinking so obsessively about it, for after all, nothing had happened, and no one had seen, and there seemed to be, between him and Mr. Tracy, a kind of agreement that they would forget about it. In each other's presence they would act as if . . . well, nothing had happened.

"Hmm! Darren."

Mr. Tracy was frowning, glancing through Darren's paper with a quivery intensity as if it merited such scrutiny. Darren stood at a distance of about three feet from him.

". . . this paper, Darren. It begins with such

promise! And then you seem to lose interest. As if . . ." Smiling nervously, and plucking at his beard, glancing up at Darren almost shyly, and quickly away again, seeing that Darren's face was tight clenched as a fist. "I really don't want to grade this paper at all, Darren. This late in the semester. What I will suggest is that you rewrite it. Entirely. No one need know. I will tear up this haphazard specimen"— briskly ripping the paper into pieces, and dropping it into a wastebasket—"and give you another chance. Due on Monday."

Darren had not expected this. He had not known what to expect, but he hadn't expected this.

The man's eager words he heard through a roaring in his ears. Must've been his blood beating hard, as it did when he was swimming underwater, clenching oxygen in his lungs.

"May I suggest, Darren: Thoreau is an anarchist. You might look up *anarchist* and define the term and discuss: What would the world be if all were anarchists? What would become of civilization without law? Thoreau is a mystic, and yet: Every man his own conscience. What would be the result of such a . . ."

Mr. Tracy's voice trailed off, uncertain. He was breathing through his mouth as if he'd been running.

Darren said no, he would not rewrite the paper.

Darren said no, thanks.

Darren backed off, frowning. He had not met Mr. Tracy's earnest gaze, and he would not now meet it.

Saying, "It wouldn't be fair that way."

"But no one need know, Darren. You've been under stress, I'm afraid, and this is a special—"

"No. It isn't. I'm not special."

"But, Darren, no one need know. Please."

"I would know, and I don't want to know."

Darren turned and walked out of the room. The roaring in his ears was so loud, he felt a momentary panic he might faint.

20

"Hey, you, watch where you're going."

"I—I'm not in your way—"

"Watch where you're looking, then. *Fag*."

It was Christmas break. They'd gone to the movies at the North Mall CineMax. This gay-boy, who Kevin swore had followed them into the men's bathroom by the escalators, was in his late twenties with a narrow, pasty face, glittering studs in his earlobes and what looked like fishhooks in his right eyebrow, right nostril and lower lip. He wore a cheaply stylish black leather jacket, tight black leather pants and black leather boots with a heel. His bleached hair lifted in moussed tufts and was shaved at the back and sides. Running a faucet at one of the sinks, Darren glanced up to see in the mirror the gay-boy looking at him with what appeared to be a sly, snaky little smile and pink tongue between his lips, and a flame passed over Darren's brain, and there was Kevin hunched at one of the urinals and Roger just zipping up, and somehow it happened, no one would know who shoved each other first, a scuffle broke out, the gay-boy was down at once on the dirty tile floor, whimpering and pleading, and Kevin cursed and kicked, and Roger cursed and kicked, and Darren did not curse but seized the gay-boy's oily hair and would've slammed his head against the concrete wall except one of his friends stopped him, and they ran, snorting with laughter, out of the bathroom and into the late-evening mall, and afterward Darren would recall as in a dream terrified eyes brimming with moisture, a bloodied nose, a torn and bloodied mouth pleading with him: *Don't! Please! Don't hurt me!*

It was past eleven P.M. The mall was nearly deserted. A middle-aged security guard started after them, calling, "Boys! Hey! Halt! Immediately!" but he was too slow and easily winded. Good luck they hadn't been wearing their purple-and-cream NFH team jackets; the guard would have recognized the school colors.

They hid behind the loading dock at Macy's. The parking lot was mostly empty. The security guard hadn't tried to follow. They would double back to Kevin's Saab when the coast was clear in a few minutes. Kevin was panting, his breath steamy in the freezing air. He laughed, blowing against his skinned knuckles.

"Oh, man! That felt good."

21

Did I want to hurt him bad? Did I want to kill him?
. . . wasn't me.

He'd be upstairs in his room. He would see head-lights turning into the driveway. He would hear a loud knock at the door.

His mother's frightened voice calling upstairs: "Darren? A police officer wants to talk to you."

Or: He's working at Pedersen's Nurseries, out-side in the Christmas-tree lot. One of several teen-aged boys Mr. Pedersen hired for the busy, blustery days preceding Christmas. And a police cruiser swings into the parking lot, and two officers get out; he's carrying an armload of evergreen wreaths to set up on display when he sees the cops conferring with

Mr. Pedersen, three adult men looking over at him, sixteen-year-old Darren Flynn wanted on suspicion of assault, and he's got a choice of surrendering or, panicked, turning to run.

    . . . wasn't me. Somebody else, not me.

22

Worked at Pedersen's through Christmas Eve, selling Christmas trees, wreaths, poinsettias. Helped his dad with household chores and repairs around the house, like tearing up the filthy old carpeting in the hall and replacing it with new. Helped his mom pick out a "complimentary" Christmas tree at the nursery, haul it home and set it up in the living room and trim it. Bought Christmas presents for his family. And for Molly Rawlings. Paying cash, counting out bills until his wallet was empty. Slept late, mornings. Some mornings, after he'd been working late at the nursery or hanging out late with his friends, he slept until noon and even then woke exhausted and dazed.

If his dad had been home, Walt Flynn would've banged on Darren's door and wakened him by nine A.M., but his mom let him sleep.

"You work hard, honey. You've been under a lot of pressure. This is your break from school; you deserve it."

Do I, Mom? How do you know what I deserve?

This past year Darren had begun to be embarrassed when his mom called him "honey." Even when no one was around to overhear. A boy of sixteen, five feet eleven, a guy's guy and no kind of *feminate,* it made him uneasy. He hadn't heard his mom call Eddy "honey" in years.

The police officers never came. There was nothing in the local news about an assault. Gay bashing, it would be called. You read about gay bashing in South Boston, Springfield. Maybe it happened in this part of New Hampshire, but you never heard about it.

Except there was Kevin cracking up the guys, even Ross Slaugh and Barry Phelps, who hadn't been there, imitating the security guard in a panting falsetto voice: "Boys! Ohhhh, boys, halt! Immediately!"

Laugh, laugh like hyenas.

Mr. Pedersen was an old friend of Walt Flynn's from high school. He worked Darren hard as a mule but was never bossy or rude to him, as some employers are to teenaged staff. Two days before Christmas, he gave Darren a surprise bonus, twenty-five dollars.

It was a great job, working outdoors in the bright fresh cold. Didn't mind the cold. Hauling Christmas trees to people's minivans, talking and laughing with families, little kids: It made Darren feel good about himself.

He wasn't a bad person. Obviously he was a good person.

Anybody who saw him at Pedersen's, they'd say, "He's a nice kid, Darren Flynn."

There were only a few scary times at the lot. Seeing a figure, a man, amid the rows of Christmas trees, or approaching through the parking lot, a red scarf or muffler around his neck, Darren came close to panicking, wanting to duck out of sight, but none of these men turned out to be Mr. Tracy, so it was OK.

Maybe he won't come back in January. Maybe he will teach somewhere else. Maybe he will disappear.

North Falls High was shut down until January. It was a weird sensation to swing by the school and see the driveways, the parking lots, front steps and front lawn heaped with fresh-fallen snow.

Wishing the snow would never be plowed away. No more school, no more bells clanging in the hallways. No more being trapped in that desk in room 208, where his legs were too long to fit. No more Mr. Tracy trying not to look at Darren, and Darren trying not to look at Mr. Tracy. Thinking: *There was nothing. It never happened. Nobody saw.*

He went with some of the guys on the team to swim at a fitness club in Hanover, where Jimmy Kovaks's father had a membership. He'd been looking forward to this, but for some reason he had trouble concentrating. Swimming laps had always been Darren's time to himself, only now his thoughts were distracted, blood pounded in his ears and he lost the rhythm of his strokes. Always he'd swum freestyle without needing to think much about it, but now he found himself thinking too much.

Climbing from the pool, streaming water and gasping for air as if he'd been punishing himself in an actual race he had neither won nor lost. Exhausting himself so that he left his thoughts behind in the sharply chlorinated water like poison that had been leached from him.

Wouldn't return to the CineMax though there were movies showing there he'd have liked to see and Molly Rawlings kept saying she'd like to see with him. Wouldn't return to the mall with his mother to exchange Christmas presents from relatives, items of clothing that didn't fit him.

The security guard hadn't seen their faces that

night, Kevin and Roger insisted. He'd only seen their backs; they'd been halfway out of the mall by the time he began chasing them.

And even if he'd seen their faces, so what?

"He wouldn't have the guts to accuse us. Not who we are. He's just a security guard, some retired cop or fuckup who couldn't get a regular job. My dad would slap a lawsuit on him, and on the mall. What could they prove? That fag couldn't identify us for sure either. He tried to, we'd say he propositioned us. His word against ours, one creepy guy against us three, who'd believe *him*?"

Kevin was boastful, sneering. Probably he was right.

Still, Darren wasn't ready to return to the mall. Not with his mother, not with Molly and, for sure, not with his friends. Remembering not the excitement he'd felt being chased by the guard but that flamelike excitement passing over his brain when he'd grabbed the guy with the nose ring by his hair, wanting to slam his head against something hard, slam and slam until there was no one seeing him out of those pleading, terrified eyes.

Christmas break. Goes on forever. You see the same people too many times. Relatives, friends. Visiting people's houses, odd times of the day. He did not open a book all during break. He wanted to, he'd meant to, promised his parents he would, but he did not. He saw his friends. He saw a lot of his friends. He saw Molly Rawlings. The evening of Christmas Day he had dinner at the Rawlingses'. They all liked him. They liked the boy they believed he was. Though Darren was quieter than usual. His mind drifted. He smiled a lot. He smiled until his face hurt. Mr. Rawlings, who was a professor at Dartmouth, always asked Darren about swimming, diving. Sports. It was what they talked about when they talked. Mrs. Rawlings asked about Darren's family.

When Darren opened Molly's present for him, there was an uneasy moment when he thought he'd opened this present before, maybe the previous

Christmas? Here at the Rawlingses'? He thanked Molly for it: a J. Crew woolen sweater, "sky blue" to match his eyes. (Darren's eyes were not sky blue but a silvery blue looking more like gray in some kinds of light.) When Molly opened the small package Darren gave her, he felt a moment of panic, not remembering what was inside.

It was a silver heart locket on a delicate silver chain. The most expensive present he'd bought this Christmas.

"Oh, Darren. It's beautiful. Thank you so much."

Molly fumbled to put it around her neck. Darren should have tried to help, but his fingers were too clumsy.

Molly kissed him suddenly. Not on the mouth but near. Meant to be spontaneous. Maybe it was. "Darren, you are the most wonderful friend . . . my closest friend." Molly laughed, blushing. "I mean, who's a boy."

Darren heard himself say, "Me too! I mean, that's how I—I feel about you."

***

Kevin's family had this so-called cabin in the White Mountains at Woodstock. Twice as big as the Flynns' house, modern in design with logs, plate glass. Stone fireplaces. Every year between Christmas and New Year's, the Pynes went skiing, and Kevin invited Darren to join them. Darren wasn't much of a skier, but it was OK, Kevin was worse. Mostly he and Kevin partied. Every night at Woodstock there were parties. You didn't need to be invited; everybody was invited. Darren met girls. Darren got drunk. Darren got high. Darren got sick to his stomach and couldn't drag himself out of bed until noon of the following day.

In this way he got through the remainder of the year.

23

It was the New Year: 2004. So much snow in early January, it was like amnesia, blinding white.

He had reason to think that things would be new, he'd have no reason to be drawn into the past. His New Year's resolution was something Coach Ellroy was always telling them: "Keep your center. In yourself. Breathe in, breathe out. Concentrate."

Hadn't spoken of his weird English teacher to anybody. Hadn't spoken to Mr. Tracy since that day back in November when he'd torn his paper into pieces and dropped them into the wastebasket.

That was how Darren mostly remembered it: He'd snatched the paper from Mr. Tracy's fingers in disgust and ripped it into pieces. Not Mr. Tracy but Darren himself had done this and felt good about it, afterward.

I'm not special. I am not.

24

There were two surprises awaiting Darren when he returned to school on January 5: He was enrolled in Ms. Katzman's junior English class, not Mr. Tracy's, which also met fifth period, and his grade for the fall term was B.

Darren stared at the printed B. Not B– but B. He felt a stab of shame; this was such a gift from his teacher.

Mr. Tracy liked to boast that he didn't hand out high grades the way you scatter birdseed. In his classes you had to work for your grade, even for a C. Darren felt the injustice, though it favored him.

The usual policy at North Falls was to continue with the same teacher you'd had first term. Mr. Tracy must have arranged for Darren to be transferred to the other junior English class, taught by

Ms. Katzman, who wasn't so flamboyant or so popular/controversial as Mr. Tracy but was a competent teacher, and not a hard grader. This too had been a gift to Darren, a parting gift.

He was so grateful! So relieved! He wouldn't have to see Mr. Tracy ever again. North Falls High was just big enough for them to avoid each other.

Darren's grades for fall term 2003 ranged from his usual A (in phys ed) to D+ (math). His other B was a B– in health, a required half-year course. When Darren's father saw his report card, he shook his head, baffled. How the hell did Darren do so well in English, where he'd always had trouble, and so poorly in math? Wasn't English a girl's subject and math a boy's?

Darren didn't speak of his grades to any of his friends. If the guys asked, he shrugged. This signaled he hadn't done very well, so fuck it.

Most of Darren's friends got C's, a few B's. All that really mattered was keeping a C– average so you wouldn't be dropped from the team.

Though she didn't tell him, Darren guessed that except for her usual B– in phys ed, Molly had straight A's. She was always high on the honor roll, though she took difficult courses like advanced French. Tactfully, Molly asked how Darren had done in Mr. Tracy's class, and Darren only just shrugged.

"But you didn't fail, Darren, did you?" Molly asked anxiously.

"No. I'm fine."

"I wish you'd let me help you more last term. Like with the Thoreau paper."

"Sure."

"It's so strange, Darren, you're in Ms. Katzman's class this term. Why, d'you think?"

"Somebody said, to even out the class lists. Mr. Tracy had more than Ms. Katzman." Darren lied smoothly, like one who's had practice.

"But I'm sorry they transferred *you*. I'll miss you."

"Yeah. I'll miss you, too."

✳✳✳

He wouldn't, though. He wouldn't miss anything about Mr. Tracy's English class. All he felt was relief, gratitude to be out of it.

25

It might've ended then. Should've ended then.

Except: ". . . so he says to see him after class. And he hands this paper back to me like it's a bad smell. And I see it's got a big fat red F on it. And I'm like really surprised saying, 'Hey, I thought I done OK on this assignment; I worked really hard.' And he says, in this prissy fag voice, 'I'm sure you worked *really hard,* Jimmy, for you. But, unfortunately, all you did was appropriate this verbiage from the ubiquitous Mr. Google.'"

It was *ver-bee-age* and *ubick-witus* Jimmy Kovaks enunciated, in an aggrieved voice. His eyes glared damply. His nostrils flared with indignation. Of the five boys crowded into the booth at McDonald's, Jimmy was the only one not actively eating. He'd chewed and swallowed a large mouthful of his cheeseburger, then set it down on his tray, leaning his elbows on the tabletop and gesturing with greasy fingers.

The other boys were Kevin Pyne, Ross Slaugh, Roger Polidari and Darren Flynn. It was late January, a Friday evening. It had been weeks since Darren had last seen Mr. Tracy. He'd been hearing that Jimmy had had some trouble with the English teacher but had not known the details. And now as Jimmy spoke, Darren lowered his eyes and listened with dread.

". . . not just Tracy gives me an F on the paper. Not just he won't let me do it over again. Won't let me explain how I was under pressure and didn't mean to take so much from the Web. See, I printed out some stuff, and it got mixed up with my own writing, kind of. I tried to explain to Tracy, and he goes, 'You plagiarized your entire paper, Jim-my. Do you think this is kindergarten? Do you think this is a game? You cheat, and I am supposed to look the other way?' And I go, 'Who're you calling a cheat, Mr. Tracy? You better not be calling me a cheat.' And—"

"You talked like that to Tracy? Wow."

"—he goes, 'A cheat is a cheat. There is no more to discuss, Jim-my.'"

Jimmy's face was so worked up, his friends were having a hard time not laughing. Jimmy banged his fist on the tabletop, scattering french fries from his tray and almost knocking over Kevin's supersize Coke. "So Tracy wants to fail me for the whole course, not just this paper, so I'm off the team for the rest of the season if he does."

Off the team. This was a death sentence.

Jimmy Kovaks was one of the team's lead swimmers. This past year he'd developed a powerful breaststroke, and his freestyle was as good as Darren's. Unlike Darren, though, Jimmy rarely suffered a lack of self-confidence; in races against really good opponents from rival schools, swimmers who were favored to win, Jimmy seemed oblivious of the situation and went all out in the final lap like a frenzied fish. Even when Jimmy Kovaks didn't actually win but came in second, he would win the crowd's admiration. You had to love a guy so fierce for winning, he wore himself out and practically had to be hauled from the pool by his teammates at the end of a race.

If any junior on the team had a chance for a sports scholarship, Darren thought it must be Jimmy.

Kevin asked if Jimmy's parents had come to talk to Tracy, and Jimmy said yes, his mother had already been in, and there was another meeting his father would attend too with the principal, Mr. Newlove.

Kevin nodded. "A father can make a big difference in leverage, a situation like that. Especially with a guy like Newlove, who wants to cover his ass."

Kevin too had been fucked over by Tracy last term. He'd just scraped through with a C–, but he'd deserved a B– at least. He had worked really hard on his term topic, but Tracy wouldn't raise his grade. "He says, 'If I raised your grade, Kev-in, I would have to raise all my students' grades in proportion. That's almost one hundred grades.' And I go, 'No, you wouldn't, Mr. Tracy! You wouldn't have to tell anyone.' And he gets this look in his face and says, 'It would be our secret, Kev-in? That's what you mean?' And I'm thinking, *This fag is falling for me, man!* and I'm like scared, but playing it cool, so I say, 'Yes, Mr. Tracy,' acting like I really, really respect him, but he just looks at me and pushes the paper back across his desk at me and says, 'I'm sorry, Kev-in. I can't raise your grade fairly, and I won't raise it unfairly. And I won't keep any transaction between myself and any student a secret."

Kevin's face was as flushed as Jimmy's. Everybody agreed it really sucked, one teacher, a fag creep like Tracy, having so much power over a guy's life.

Kevin turned unexpectedly to Darren, who'd been quiet through much of the conversation. "Darren, he fucked you over too, didn't he? How'd you do in English?"

Darren, taken by surprise, still knew to shrug instinctively and assume a look of sullen indifference. Kevin and the others already knew, or thought they knew, that Darren's grades last term hadn't been anything to brag about. They wouldn't push it now. Darren Flynn was one of them.

Talk turned to whether Tracy was actually a fag.

"He ain't married, is he?"

"So what if he was? That doesn't prove anything. Lots of guys you hear about, married guys, a certain age, they turn queer."

"They *do*? Hey, not my dad!"

"Not our dads. But y'know, other old guys. They get to be like forty . . ."

"This Tracy, he's strange! He's got this dog he walks, this little spaniel. Some kind of chevalier something. That's a queer breed, you just know. He lives on my aunt's street; she sees him. Acts like he's some kind of, y'know—aristocrat. Fancy words he uses, always acting so superior. He really gets off on putting a guy down. Girls, he likes. A girl like Molly

Rawlings. You can see he favors them. The weird thing is, Tracy follows some sports. He comes to our meets. He's got this cool digital camera; he takes pictures during a meet. But like, in class, it's like he's got something against athletes. He treats us like anybody else." Roger Polidari spoke with an air of mounting reproach. "Guys playing football, guys who won the district basketball title last year, to guys like us he says, 'I don't make exceptions.' It was an actual thing Tracy said, a prissy little speech, in our English class last year."

By this time Barry Phelps and Drake Hardin had joined the boys, dragging chairs to the booth. Barry was a tall, lanky basketball player, excitable and loudly sympathetic. Drake was a quieter boy, with dark quill-like hair sprouting from a low forehead. Like Darren, Drake lived outside North Falls but had managed to attach himself to the popular in crowd. Unlike Darren, Drake was not especially popular himself, not a very nice guy, one of the weaker varsity basketball players.

Thrown together, Drake and Darren were civil with each other. But Darren knew that Drake talked about him behind his back, ridiculed his father's work ("'Roadkill Patrol'! Cool!"). Darren never saw Drake without thinking, *He hates my guts.*

Barry said, spraying spittle in his excitement, "Yeah! Tracy's got a grudge against us. You could prove it by statistics. Like half the basketball team was under threat of suspension last year because of him? Girls' field hockey, those dykes he goes for. He don't discriminate against them, huh? Well, why not? But any guy like us, he's got this bias. Jimmy, you need to argue 'bias.' Get your dad to threaten a lawsuit, I'm serious."

Jimmy said, disgusted, "Like sue for what? The bastard printed out the Web crap that's like all my paper, that I got from four or five sites, but the fucker found 'em all. He says it's 'proof positive.' It's 'plag-rism,' he said, he won't raise the F."

"If Newlove tells him to, he has to, don't he? Newlove's the principal. Tracy's ass can be fired."

"Newlove won't. He won't want trouble like in the media."

"He's got trouble. *His* ass can be fired too."

"Like these old farts playing God! Like they fuck up a guy's professional career."

By this time Jimmy had become really agitated. Moisture shone in his eyes. As in the pool he exhibited spurts of sudden manic energy, like small explosions, so in the company of sympathetic friends he came alive in spurts of indignation; he was moved by his own misery. Bawling, "The worst thing! Guys, want to hear the worst thing!" and his friends said, "Yes, what's the worst thing?" and Jimmy said, lips trembling, "Coach is pissed with me! Coach is pissed with me! I told him about the jam I was in, he goes to talk to Tracy, and Tracy shows him the 'proof positive,' and now Coach is pissed with me. Saying how could I be such an asshole, so stupid, 'plag-rizing' off the Web like that, stupid enough to think a genius-IQ guy like Tracy wouldn't know where it came from?" Jimmy sighed, grimacing. Lifted his cooling cheeseburger to his mouth to take an enormous bite and repeat, through a full mouth, "Oh, man, can you believe! Coach is pissed with *me*."

26

Weeks later Darren would realize: *That was it. That night. The beginning.*

He'd been powerless to stop it; what could he have done?

Nothing Darren Flynn could have done.

Nothing Darren Flynn could have said.

In fact what Darren said was, wiping ketchup from his mouth with a soiled napkin, breaking into the raucous conversation among his friends, "Tracy's taking digital pictures? Of guys in Speedos? Somebody should look into that."

27

A week following the evening at McDonald's, there was Coach glaring at them. Fixing his furious gaze upon them. Saying in a voice of utter disgust, "Kovaks is off the team for the rest of the season. Word just came from the front office. The final word. No more appeals."

Coach paused. You could see a vein pulsing in his dome of a forehead. It was no surprise about Kovaks since Kovaks wasn't with them this afternoon. Yet the air quivered with strain, dread.

"Know whose fault that is? Why Kovaks is off the team?"

No one dared speak. Darren was hugging his bare knees, shivering. The chlorine smell you don't have time to notice when you're swimming laps was oppressive now, like a toxic gas.

"Pyne? You're smirking. You're a buddy of Kovaks's, you got something to tell us?"

Kevin laughed nervously. Kevin mumbled something inaudible.

"Got bubble gum in your mouth, Pyne? Speak up."

"I said, 'Mr. T-Tracy did it. It's his fault about Jimmy."

"'Mr. T-Tracy.'" Coach spoke with yet more disgust. Almost you might think he was enjoying this. It wasn't like Kevin to stammer, but confronted by Coach, even a hard-nosed guy like Kevin could lose his cool. "No. It was not the fault of 'Mr. T-Tracy.' It was Jimmy Kovaks's own fault. He's off the team, he's let his teammates down, he's screwed us for the rest of the season because of something he did, himself. Got it? All of you?" Coach drew himself up to his full height (which wasn't so tall, maybe six feet one), standing with his hands on his hips like an army drill sergeant. "Something Kovaks did, of his own free will. Your buddy KO-VAKS."

Coach had more to say, you could see his mouth working, but he turned abruptly and walked away. In his memory Darren would see the man limping, wounded.

28

At first it was on Jimmy Kovaks's behalf. And on behalf of the swim team. Then, as word spread through North Falls High, rapacious as wildfire in dry grass, other grudges against the English teacher were voiced.

He failed me!

He failed *me*!

There were seniors smarting from low grades they'd gotten from Tracy the previous year. There was the junior class treasurer who hated Tracy for giving him a B– and "sabotaging" his 3.9 grade point average. There were football players Tracy had "dissed," and there was Roger Polidari with a D– on his most recent written assignment in Tracy's class: "And it wasn't 'plag-rized,' either. It was my own shit."

There was Barry Phelps, who insisted that Tracy had a "bias" against athletes and "had to be eliminated."

There was Drake Hardin, who had never been a student of Tracy's but was unquestioningly loyal to his friend Barry.

And always there seemed to be Kevin Pyne.

Not serious. Just talk. Bullshitting.
. . . I don't need to know.

Why'd Darren Flynn need to know, even to listen to his friends plotting revenge against Mr. Tracy?

(Which was what they called it: "revenge"— "vengeance.")

(Like some video game for junior high–aged kids. Nonstop WHAM WHAM WHAM BOOMBOOM!)

Darren was in another English class now, and grateful. When talk swerved onto Tracy, the latest wisecrack he'd made to someone, the latest low grade he'd given to someone who'd deserved higher, a weird and farfetched rumor of Tracy cruising the gay bar scene (in Burlington, Vermont?) or the video arcade at the North Falls Mall (?), Darren's mind drifted off. Sometimes he left his friends, with the excuse he had work to do: like at lunch in the cafeteria when the guys' table got really crowded, twelve, fifteen guys noisy and laughing, drawing the attention of others.

Envious attention, Darren knew.

Eyes on him, too: Darren Flynn. *Is Darren Flynn cool! Oh, man, is Darren Flynn good-looking!*

He had to admit, he liked being envied. It pumped you up when you were down. It made your walk a little springier, inspired you to hold your head a little higher than you'd have done, probably, if you were alone and no one was watching.

29

"We miss you, Darren. In English class."

Darren's face reddened. He wasn't about to ask Molly if Mr. Tracy had actually said he missed him.

In Ms. Katzman's class, Darren's grades were generally good. It was known that Ms. Katzman was a much easier grader than Mr. Tracy. It was known that Ms. Katzman's class was S L O W. You could digest your lunch, dozing off. Ms. Katzman was a stout woman with a dropsical bosom and a hurt little smile. One of those no-name teachers you like OK but forget as soon as you're out of their classroom.

Darren was surprised how little anyone had to say in Ms. Katzman's class. They were using the same literature anthology Mr. Tracy used, *American Vistas*, but there wasn't much discussion about anything they read, and there were never any disagreements. Nothing seemed to matter much. Who cared about characters in fiction, or what Robert Frost really meant by "The Road Not Taken"? Ms. Katzman was a practical person, a veteran teacher older than Mr. Tracy, who used up class time outlining plots and "themes" to prepare her students for the statewide standardized final exam in June. Darren remarked to Molly that the minute hand of the clock in his new teacher's classroom moved twice as slowly as the minute hand of the clock in Mr. Tracy's classroom.

Molly said, "Sounds like you miss us too, Darren."

30

. . . see, he's a fag. You can tell by just looking at him.

A fag gets what he deserves. He's begging for it.

"Pervert"—"peophile"—

"*Ped*ophile"—

Like those Catholic priests you hear about, they go after young kids.

Tracy's the enemy; he's got a "bias."

He's the enemy, not us.

A secret life, you can tell. They all do.

Sure he's careful around here. Knows what would happen to him if he got caught.

He looks at you funny, though.

(Never came on to any guy at school? Never once?)

(Not that anybody knows. So far.)

***

It was Kevin's original idea. Get some gay porn, some kiddie porn if they could find it, mark it up and leave it for Tracy to find like on his desk at school, or on the windshield of his car, so he'd know his secret was out. It was Drake Hardin's idea not to leave the porn for Tracy, who'd only get rid of it and be tipped off he was outed, but to put it in a sealed envelope and address it to Principal Newlove with a message it's from some fucked-up sex-molested victim of Tracy's: "See, that gets him in trouble. He won't even know about it until Newlove calls him in. He's the one who gets fucked."

Darren had not known about this. Not exactly.

Anyway, the guys were just talking. Bullshitting. You couldn't take any of it seriously.

Can't get involved.

Sometime in February they got hold of the magazines. Tore out certain of the full-color photo features, practically gagging, this stuff was so disgusting. Naked boys, and naked men. But mostly naked boys. Some of the boys looked really young. It was so disgusting! Truly sicko stuff so shocking to a normal straight guy, it made the back of his neck stand up, made him want to puke.

Anybody got turned on by this stuff, he was truly SICKO.

Truly SICKO and not deserving to live.

In all there were maybe ten, twelve pulp photos. They were loose in a manila envelope addressed to "JOHN NEWLOVE, PRINCIPLE NORTH FALLS HIGH SCHOOL." Included with the photos was a childishly handprinted message in red pencil on a sheet of torn notebook paper:

MR. TARCY HAS MAD ME SICK TO LIV
I AM SOASHAMED HAVING TO SEE THIS
I AM NOT IN YR SCHOOL. I AM 11 YRS OLD
I WOULD LIKE KILL MYSELF

Sometime after five P.M. on February 11, 2004, this (sealed) manila envelope was shoved beneath Principal Newlove's office door by Kevin Pyne in the company of three friends: Roger Polidari, Barry Phelps, Drake Hardin. The boys then walked un-hurriedly away along the partly darkened, deserted corridor and left the school. They were nerved up, excited. They were maybe just slightly scared. These were boys made canny from watching crime programs on TV; they knew not to leave fingerprints on any of the pieces of paper, and no one had been stupid enough to lick the glue on the manila envelope seal and leave any trace of DNA. They had not used any computer to print out the message, knowing that computer printers can be traced. Kevin Pyne was their leader. Kevin Pyne was the dominant conspir-ator, the boy who had hand-printed the message in red pencil and had, with the help of the others, thought up the inspired contents of the message. But it was Drake Hardin who said, as they were climbing into Kevin's Saab, "Shit! We should've sent it to the police."

And Kevin Pyne said, turning the key in the igni-tion, calm as if he'd been thinking this himself, "We can. Next time."

31

Two weeks later there was Eddy leaning in Darren's doorway, fixing him with a funny look.

"Who's your English teacher, bro?"

Darren told him. The same teacher Eddy had had a few years ago, Katzman.

Eddy was mildly disappointed. "Oh, her. I kind of forgot her name."

It was late in the Flynns' household, past eleven P.M. Eddy had to get up at six A.M. but had been out with his girlfriend, Ruthie, hadn't had supper at home and Darren could smell beer on his breath and a yeasty-perfumy odor he guessed was Eddy's girlfriend's odor that made Darren feel sexy and resentful at the same time.

"Why're you asking about my English teacher?"

"'Cause I been hearing some pretty heavy stuff

about some other English teacher there. Guy who came after I graduated, I guess."

Darren was very still. Knowing, if he showed the slightest surprise or an active interest, that Eddy would become evasive.

That was Eddy's way: tease, tantalize. Always he seemed bemused by his younger brother's earnestness. As he was irritated by their mother's concern for him and their father's disappointment.

". . . can't say his name, it's confidential. For now. There's something sicko going on at the school, just maybe."

Quickly Darren thought: One of his brother's friends was a young police officer with the North Falls PD. It must be from Eddy's police friend he'd heard news of an investigation of some kind. . . .

Sicko. Had to mean sex. Sick sex, pervert sex.

Eddy said, "You don't seem too interested, bro. You're looking kind of doubtful."

Darren laughed. Tried to sound convincing.

Like someone who'd naturally think his brother had to be joking.

Darren was slumped at his makeshift, cluttered desk. Not an actual desk, but a solid squat table of untreated pine Darren's father had built for him years before. Darren was trying, through a mild-headache haze, to make sense of some chemistry equations; there was a test coming up on Friday. (It was Wednesday now. If he was in trouble, he'd better know what to ask in school tomorrow.) But Darren was flashing on swim practice that afternoon, how he'd started off impressively with his backstroke (the best stroke: Your face is out of the water, you can breathe without calculation), then he'd gotten distracted, and his freestyle was choppy, and Coach hadn't said much about his diving except "Keep it up, Darren; you're getting there." Sort of sighing, like Coach was pushing a heavy weight up a hill. Since Kovaks was off the team, it seemed like some spirit had departed. Kovaks was noisy, explosive, erratic, but you missed him.

North Falls had narrowly lost a meet against White River High they should have won. And tougher competition was scheduled for March.

Mr. Tracy was being blamed for sure. No matter what Coach Ellroy had said. It was noticeable that the English teacher hadn't attended the meet with White River.

Hadn't dared. He'd have been booed.

Or worse.

Darren hadn't been told what exactly was being done by Kevin and the others, or had already been done. He'd allowed his friends to know that he was out of it.

Didn't want to be part of it. Whatever it was.

(Though knowing that Drake Hardin was involved, with Kevin. The two were getting tight now. Talking together at Kevin's locker, laughing. Plotting.)

Another reason Darren was finding it hard to concentrate this evening: There were a half dozen e-mail messages from girls he had not gotten around to answering, including Molly Rawlings, who was always sending him bright little one-liners like a bird chirping in a corner of his room: "Hi, Darren! Missed you at school today."

Not that Darren was avoiding Molly. Just he seemed always to be forgetting her.

Eddy had been talking with teasing vagueness about the "confidential"—"sicko"—"underground stuff" at Darren's school, in an effort to stir Darren's curiosity. But Darren just laughed, shook his head as if this had to be ridiculous. Eddy finally said, with an odd, unexpected tenderness, "You're a good kid, bro. You take things serious the way they should be."

This strange remark from his brother Darren would long remember.

As he would remember the date: February 25, 2004.

32

Wouldn't think of it. He would not.

Too much to think about, his own life. *A good kid* his brother believed him, and so did others, plenty of others. At school he had no reason to see Mr. Tracy ever, not ever again. Ms. Katzman's classroom was just above the stairs; Mr. Tracy's was at the farther end of the corridor.

On Monday the first of the rumors surfaced. Something weird was going on, but what, exactly? Some kind of "investigation"—"secret meetings" in Mr. Newlove's office? A student assistant in the library told her friends she'd overheard two librarians talking of someone about to take a "medical leave"— maybe for a "nervous breakdown"?

Mr. Tracy was spoken of, often. Where in the past his classroom remarks and witticisms were repeated to be laughed over and admired, now it was reported he was looking "nervous," "distracted," "kind of disheveled, like he'd gotten dressed in the dark."

Molly Rawlings remarked to Darren, "He's talking to us, and his eyes are sort of edging toward the door, like he expects somebody to come in. He'll be talking and forget what he's saying; it's so sad. Then he gets all energetic and excited again and keeps talking past the bell like he hasn't heard it and we're just sitting there, not wanting to be rude and leave. . . . There was just a poem of his in *The New Yorker*; my mother saved it for me. It's beautiful but kind of mysterious. See?"

Molly took a folded-over sheet of thin paper from her bag, but Darren hadn't time to read the poem. Not just then.

33

"Darren? Telephone."

It was Darren's mother, calling to him in the driveway. He'd been dragging empty trash cans back to the carport. Wearing just a flannel shirt and jeans, and it was like twenty-five degrees Fahrenheit.

A call? Telephone?

Quickly Darren reasoned: None of his friends would call him at that number. Not his parents' number. Darren had his own line, and anyway, his friends would e-mail.

"Ask who it is, Mom?"

Darren finished dragging the trash cans against the side of the house. Big, ugly, clumsy orange crude plastic cans that were badly stained and smelly. Darren's heart was beating hard; he had an athlete's instinctive wariness. You had to protect yourself, had to be alert and prepared.

When he went inside the house, his mother told him whoever it was hadn't left his name or his number.

"Not one of your girlfriends this time," his mother said, teasing. "Some man, I think. Sounded older."

Darren shrugged and was out of the kitchen.

Wouldn't think of it. Would not.

34

That night there was a message from *ltracy:*

March 5, 2004

Dear Darren,

Will you call me as soon as you receive this?

I am not comfortable calling you.

This is an urgent matter. My number is . . .

Lowell Tracy

Darren did not call the number. Darren did not reply to the e-mail message. Darren pressed Delete.

35

March 6, 2004

Dear Darren,

I am appealing to you though I realize it is a very great favor to ask of a high school boy.

Will you speak as a "character witness" on my behalf? I will provide more details, of course. But please know that your remarks would be held in the strictest confidence.

Lowell Tracy

Darren read this message several times. His heart was beating so hard, he panicked that he might faint.

It was like drowning, choking. Your mouth, nose, lungs filling up with water like furious snakes rushing inside you.

He pressed Delete. He clicked off his e-mail. He shut down his clunky old computer for the night.

36

March 7, 2003

Dear Darren,

This will be my final appeal, I promise.

I am appealing to you as your former teacher and, I hope, a friend.

I am appealing to you as one who is being cruelly and crudely investigated by local law enforcement officers and other so-called professionals intent upon exacting from me a ridiculous confession to crimes I did not commit nor ever contemplated committing against young people like you. I am fighting to maintain my professional career as I am being pressured by school officials to take a temporary medical leave from teaching to avert a "possible scandal."

All I ask of you, Darren, is to speak briefly on my behalf as a character witness. You would only say the truth to the biased and ignorant police officers intent upon destroying me and to the cowardly John Newlove, principal of North Falls High, and the craven and duplicitous legal counsel assigned by the North Falls Board of Education to this case.

All you need to tell them, Darren, is that I am not a teacher who has betrayed his trust. I am not a person who has "preyed upon" his students.

For I AM NOT! I think that you know I AM NOT.

I have continued to teach for the past week under increasing pressure. I don't know how long I can endure this persecution. I have tried to behave as if nothing has wounded me. As if I have not been accused of terrible things by unnamed sources.

Will you help me, Darren? Only a word from you, who are so highly regarded at the school and would make such a fine impression on those who wish to make me their enemy.

(I am writing this very late at night, as I would not perhaps be capable of writing it by day.)

Sincerely,

Lowell Tracy

37

March 8, 2004

Dear Mr. Tracy,

All right. I will. I can say that you were the best teacher I had at NFH. There was nothing outside of class that I know of. Thats all I can say.

Sincerely,

Darren Flynn

. . . woke tangled in damp bedclothes. His breath ragged and hurting as if he'd been swimming against a tough current. He was baffled to discover he'd fallen asleep still dressed, only his shoes off. It was still dark outside. It was five forty a.m. His table lamp was on; weird he hadn't switched it off. His computer screen saver glowed. He stumbled to check his e-mail, dreading what he would find, and there was the pathetic message he'd typed out so slowly and painfully hours before and had not sent.

All right. I will. I can say that you were

He moved the cursor onto Send. He hesitated; his heart was pounding like something trapped in his chest.

Do you want. Your name linked with. Character witness. Don't get involved. Asshole!

He moved the cursor to Delete.

Are you sure, Y/N?

Y. He was sure.

38

Following this, things happened swiftly.

On Monday morning, Mr. Tracy's several English classes were met by Mr. Newlove, who grimly announced that Mr. Tracy was on "indefinite medical leave" and introduced them to the nervously smiling young woman substitute teacher who was taking his place.

The young woman substitute appeared to know nothing about Mr. Tracy. Partway into the first class, a boy raised his hand to ask if it was true what people were saying, Mr. Tracy had been "arrested for some kind of sex crime," and the young woman stared at him astonished as the class erupted into nervous laughter.

"Ms. Katzman? Do you know what happened to Mr. Tracy?"

"No. I most certainly do not."

In Ms. Katzman's drowsy fifth-period English class, this was the only exchange that aroused interest.

Lifting his eyes to his teacher's face, Darren saw something prim and satisfied there. *She's glad. She hates him. She's jealous of him.*

Where Mr. Tracy was, no one knew. After school several carloads of students drove past his house on Meridian Avenue, where he rented the upstairs, but the venetian blinds on all the second-floor windows were drawn.

"Maybe he's hiding inside?"

"Nah, he's gone. I bet."

"I thought he was arrested?"

"So? He'd be out on bail."

In fact Lowell Tracy had not been arrested. Calls made by agitated parents to the North Falls Police Department were routed to a woman officer, who explained in a cordial voice that "no information is being released at the present time" about Lowell Tracy.

Questions about an investigation into "some kind of gay sex crimes" were met with a cordial but firm "No comment."

Darren hadn't been among the boys who'd driven past Mr. Tracy's house. He hadn't been among the boys who'd driven past the house honking horns, circling the block and driving past again in a mood of hilarity. He'd known that they were going, though. He'd said, frowning, "Maybe you guys should let him alone. It's gone far enough."

Kevin said innocently, "Let what alone? What's gone far enough?"

"You know."

"Know what? Who knows? *You?*"

"Coach said it wasn't his fault . . ."

"What wasn't whose fault? You got bubble gum in your mouth, Flynn?"

Mocking, Kevin cupped his hand against his ear.

Darren shoved at him, would have punched him except Kevin backed off, laughing. The other guys intervened. It was over within seconds. A flaring match shaken out. Darren found himself walking quickly and blindly away, pushing through a door to the outside.

With Kevin were Roger Polidari, Jimmy Kovaks, Barry Phelps, and Drake Hardin. He knew they were watching him go, smirking. He knew they were laughing at him.

Seemed like Drake was always with the guys now. Tight with Kevin Pyne as he was with Barry Phelps.

Bastards. Hate their guts.

". . . there's this list, see. Mr. Tracy's 'victims.' Most of them are real young kids like in grade school. My aunt says there's a nine-year-old boy in the house next door to his . . ."

"This list! You heard there's six guys on it, from our school?"

"Six? I heard ten."

". . . guys you wouldn't expect. Like, guys on the swim team? Kovaks, Polidari, Pyne . . ."

"Bullshit, they're not gay."

"Not that they're gay, but Tracy came on to them. Tried to blackmail them with grades."

"Pyne is testifying to the cops. Nobody's supposed to know."

"District attorney, I heard."

". . . if there's a trial."

"You think there's gonna be a trial?"

"Drake Hardin says Tracy came on to him one night, out at the mall. Like, Drake says, the fag didn't recognize him from school, didn't know who he was, kind of bumping against him in a bathroom, and making goo-goo eyes in the mirror . . ."

"Drake Hardin! That asshole."

"Shows you how desperate Tracy is. I mean, was."

On the morning of March 11, Mr. Newlove announced at a specially convened assembly that there were "absolutely no grounds" for rumors that Mr. Tracy had been dismissed from the North Falls School District.

"As I thought I'd made clear, Mr. Tracy is on indefinite medical leave. More than that I can't tell you. He will possibly return before the end of the term; that is quite possible." But Mr. Newlove spoke haltingly, as if something were caught in his throat.

39

". . . at your school, some kind of gay sex crimes investigation; what's going on?"

"I don't really know, Dad. There's a lot of talk but . . ."

"Some of your friends are involved? Is that possible?"

"Dad, no. Not really."

" 'Not really'? What the hell does that mean?"

". . . I mean really, no. They are not involved."

"They're giving testimony to the police, is what I hear."

It was like a gang hit. Walt Flynn had asked Darren to ride out with him to the lumberyard, where he was making some purchases. And this was so, Walt was buying asphalt siding, but also he had questions he wanted to put to Darren out of the house, where Darren's mother wouldn't hear.

"You know how upset your mother gets. Emotional. And this sick stuff, this secret gay sex stuff, she's been hearing from her friends every time the phone rings, and I've been hearing. And what I need to know, Darren, is—"

"I told you, Dad. I don't know."

"I called Kevin Pyne's father. *He* wasn't friendly."

"You called Kevin's father? Why?"

"Because Kevin's name is being mentioned. Because he's been seen at the police station. Because you and him are friends. That's why."

"What did Mr. Pyne say?"

"Mr. Pyne said, 'I can't discuss this matter. I'm hanging up now.'" Walt Flynn cursed, calling the man a word Darren had never heard his father speak before.

"I wish you hadn't called Mr. Pyne, Dad. He has nothing to do with—"

"With what? What?"

"With anything."

"With anything *what*?"

"I told you, Dad. I don't know. There's all this bullshit crap people are saying at school . . ."

"This teacher, Tracy, he was your teacher last semester? How'd that go?"

"Fine."

"What's he like?"

". . . just a teacher. He's OK."

A brooding, guarded look came into Walt Flynn's eyes. He said, clearing his throat, "He's—feminite, is he? Femin*ate*?"

Darren shrugged. This was such a nightmare, he was fearful of laughing.

"I mean, like, you know—gay?"

Darren was looking blank. Clenching his jaws as he'd done in school so many times, back in middle school especially. Trying not to laugh like hell so the arteries in your head are practically bursting.

"You got a B in English, Darren. That's pretty good, eh?"

"I guess."

"What?"

"I said, yeah, I guess."

"For you. Mostly you get C's."

His dad's emphasis on *you*. Wasn't too subtle. Like saying, "You are so stupid, how'd you get anything higher than C?"

"You want me to apologize, Dad? For not getting a C?"

"Look, don't you get smart with me, Darren. This isn't the time."

"I'm not! I—"

"There's nothing more to it than that, is there?"

"Than what?"

"Don't play dumb with me! I'm not your adoring mother. You're telling me you got a B in fucking English, I never got any B in fucking English, and Eddy got a D. So I'm wondering."

"Dad, I don't know what the hell you're wondering. This is making me feel like puking."

"*You! You* feel like puking, what about me! I'm your fucking father."

Darren bit his lower lip hard.

Better not laugh. Oh, man!

"See, Darren, some of the guys were saying today at work, the kids who are testifying are 'lawyered up.' These rich kids. Whatever comes down, they'll be protected. Their names won't be in the papers or on TV, you bet. But a kid like you . . ."

"Me? What about me? Is somebody talking about *me?*"

"That's what I'm wondering, Darren."

"Dad, why'd they be talking about *me?* I didn't go to the police. I got nothing to say to cops."

Walt regarded his son glumly. "OK. But if I hear you're involved in this sicko stuff somehow, some way . . ."

Darren jammed his fist against his mouth; laughter was bubbling up like vomit. They'd been parked for ten minutes at least on a rutted access road beyond the lumberyard. His dad's mud-splattered '93 Chevy pickup was the kind of rust bucket you could die of carbon monoxide in, the motor running in cold weather. Darren was trying to keep his mouth shut. His dad would slap him silly if he gave in to a fit of laughing, worse yet vomiting. He was feeling really shaky, weird. Wished he had someone to talk to about this, but there wasn't anybody left.

Thinking, *Mr. Tracy might've understood. Too late now.*

Shut his eyes, feeling weak. Sinking to the bottom of the pool like a waterlogged body defeated by gravity, and still, his old man was scolding like Coach yelling at him to get his ass out of the water, stop screwing around.

40

March 14, 2004

kev whats this bullshit u r talking to
COPS??? whats this LIST people r talking
about? we need to talk

darren

Kevin must not have thought so, though. Didn't
return Darren's e-mail and didn't call.

41

. . . sighting Kevin in the junior corridor, at his locker. Seeing how Kevin glanced in Darren's direction nervously, defiantly. Darren slammed his locker shut. Darren pulled his grungy baseball cap on his head. Darren pushed through swarms of students to get to Kevin before Kevin could escape.

Without the other guys, Kevin wasn't so cocky.

"My dad says you're talking to *cops*? You are?"

Kevin shrugged evasively.

"About Mr. Tracy? You're testifying about Mr. Tracy? What the hell do you know about Mr. Tracy?"

Darren was attracting attention in the corridor. But Darren was oblivious of anyone else.

Kevin said, "Not so loud, Darren. Jesus!"

Kevin was nearly as tall as Darren but thicker in the torso and shoulders. His face was a pouty baby face with oddly bristling eyebrows.

". . . this list, see? Somebody gave it to the NFPD. Somebody made a complaint against Tracy a few weeks ago; he's showing gay porn to young kids. Hangs around video arcades. Some kid in junior high he was messing with tried to kill himself. The cops have got to investigate to see how many kids have been molested. Look," Kevin said, uncomfortable with Darren standing so close to him, "this shit got out of hand. It was kind of a joke, y'know, at first. I mean, me and Jimmy weren't serious. I mean, we were pissed off at Tracy, sure, but we weren't, like, serious about . . ." Kevin's voice grew vague. He was backing off from Darren. "See, there's this list. The cops got it from somewhere. Not me! They ask you names, names of other guys Tracy might've come on to, but I didn't give up any names, I swear! Jimmy thinks it was Newlove, or the school shrink here, trying to 'cooperate.' They're calling guys in, over at police headquarters, they keep it 'confidential.' It isn't so bad actually. They respect you. You can have a lawyer if you want one. You can have your dad or mom with you. See, we're minors, we can't be questioned like adults." Kevin laughed nervously, wiping his nose with his fist.

Darren was feeling sick. Wondering if he could believe anything Kevin said. Wanting so badly to punch Kevin that his fists clenched.

"You didn't give them my name, did you?"

"I said no! I didn't give anybody any names; they already had them."

There came Ross Slaugh swinging by, thumping Darren on the shoulder. They'd been friends since fifth grade; Ross was OK. And there was Mikey Eimer, a short, nervy kid with a wrestler's body. Guys Darren had known for years, guys he'd grown up with. They were on their way to the cafeteria for lunch.

"You coming, Flynn? C'mon."

"Can't. Thanks."

The guys left. Kevin didn't look back. The corridor was emptying out. Darren stood unmoving.

There was a school regulation about baseball caps worn indoors, but Darren had jammed his Red Sox cap down onto his forehead; the rim was cutting into his skin.

A list! *Darren Flynn* would be on that list.

It was one week since Mr. Tracy had "disappeared" from North Falls High. Darren was wishing he could disappear too.

42

Darren swallowed hard. He knew.

As soon as he came home. Through the rear door into the brightly lit kitchen where Mom was preparing dinner. Swinging his backpack onto a chair, blinking moisture from his eyes after the harsh, cold, wet wind. There was Mom looking at him with this expression he had not seen on her face in years: anxious as if her child had fallen, had hurt himself badly.

". . . a call from the North Falls Police Department? A detective who says he wants to t-talk with you? Oh, Darren."

Darren was unzipping his waterproof jacket. Tossed it onto the bench beside the back door, where newspapers and other flat paper trash accumulated.

"Hey, Mom. I didn't kill anybody."

Darren laughed. A hoarse, phony laugh. His mother stood staring at him as if wondering whether he told the truth.

It was late, going on six P.M. Darren was relieved his father's pickup wasn't in the driveway.

Eddy wasn't home yet, either. Just Mom.

Tell her. Tell her everything.

. . . nothing to tell! There was nothing.

The ride home with Mr. Tracy that night. Stopping at the Coffee Cowboy. Mr. Tracy's edgy, nervous, excited chatter, which Darren had scarcely heard. All that Mr. Tracy had done, or said, that was maybe inappropriate was asking Darren to call him by his first name. . . .

But he'd immediately retracted the request. Almost, Darren could pretend he had not heard.

"There was nothing. I mean, *nothing*."

"Darren, what?"

"There isn't anything. For them to ask me."

"But what is going on, Darren? The detective wouldn't explain. He just said to call back, to arrange for a time to come to police headquarters. I've been hearing such strange, upsetting things, Darren; everyone is talking about—"

"It's bullshit, Mom. Like I said, it's *nothing*."

"Darren, how do you know?"

Rubbed his knuckles against his eyes. How did he know? Well—he knew.

But how did he *know*? Lowell Tracy might have been leading a secret life, in fact.

Darren had stayed after school to swim laps. No official practice for the team that afternoon; only a few swimmers and none of them close friends of his. He'd been so charged up, he'd had to swim laps for forty minutes virtually without resting. Snorting and gasping for air like a beached porpoise. The other swimmers, some of them girls, had observed Darren with admiration, awe, amusement, then with mounting concern. *Darren! That's enough, better stop.*

He'd staggered from the pool exhausted. His eyes were reddened; he was nauseated from swallowing water.

"Dad doesn't know? Yet?"

"No. He'll be home soon, though."

"I guess . . . do we have to tell him?"

"Darren, of course! We couldn't keep such a . . ." Mom paused, wiping at her eyes. ". . . a thing from him. Dad would know."

This was true; Walt Flynn would know.

In North Falls, population 8,300, news traveled fast. Disturbing news, bad news, disaster news and humiliating news, really fast.

"Don't look so worried, Darren. Your father could come with you, or I could. The detective said it might inhibit you from saying all that you know, but it's allowed; you're a minor."

43

In the morning Darren checked his e-mail. A message had come during the night from *ltracy*.

Tracy had said he wouldn't! Wouldn't write to Darren again.

"I hate him. Wish he'd leave me alone . . ."

March 16, 2004

Dear Darren,

Forgive me, I promised I would not appeal to you again. But I have heard that you may be interviewed soon by North Falls detectives!

Please speak on my behalf, Darren. You

need only tell the truth. I always respected
and

Darren clicked Delete, quickly. The message was
so very long.

44

The look on Walt Flynn's face! But he'd believed Darren—there was nothing to any of this.

Wanted to believe, anyway.

The one who'd really looked stunned was Eddy.

As if half believing—what? His younger brother might be gay?

"Hey, bro, it's just, like, a formality," Darren said, swallowing hard. "Lots of guys are being called in, I guess."

Eddy ran a hand through his spiky hair. He hadn't shaved for twelve hours and was looking pretty scruffy.

"Sure, Darren. Right."

"I mean, the guys on the team are being called

in. It doesn't mean anything."

Eddy tried to smile. Eddy was trying to look as if he believed his younger brother, Darren.

45

They can't force me. They don't know anything.

There wasn't anything.

He was frightened, and he was resentful. But he told his parents he'd go to police headquarters alone. He didn't need a ride, and he didn't need anyone with him: "Hey, I'm sixteen. Not six."

His appointment with Detective Forrester was for four P.M., March 18. He hiked downtown from school, a distance of about a mile.

The school day had passed in a haze of distraction. Darren had to wonder if people were looking at him strangely. Even Molly Rawlings. His teachers. In the corridor outside the principal's office, there was Mr. Newlove with his forced-friendly smile and anxious eyes, nodding hello.

All of them wondering, *Is Darren Flynn on the list?*

The rumor was that Mr. Tracy was "away."

No; Mr. Tracy was "hiding out" in his place on Meridian Avenue.

The rumor was that Mr. Tracy had failed a polygraph test given by the North Falls police.

No; Mr. Tracy had passed a polygraph test.

The rumor was that over the last several days, Mr. Tracy had been calling and e-mailing students "appealing" to them for help. . . .

Darren never asked about his former teacher. He had to wonder uneasily if he was the only person in all of North Falls who never asked.

"Darren Flynn? Come in and have a seat, please."

His heart was pounding as if he'd climbed up onto the high board, but Detective Forrester was a friendly-seeming man, peering at Darren above the lenses of his reading glasses, and Detective Tyding was a smiling woman of about Darren's mother's age, with stylishly clipped bleached hair dark at the roots. Kevin had said the detectives treated you respectfully, and so it seemed to Darren, at least at first.

46

FLYNN, DARREN JAMES.
16, junior, North Falls High School.

ADDRESS: *Route 11, Box 182, North Falls,*
New Hampshire.
PARENTS: *Walter and Edith Flynn.*
RELATIONSHIP TO L. TRACY: *former student.*
INTERVIEWS WITH: *Detectives Forrester,*
Tyding. 3/18/04, 3/19/04.

Did he ever approach you suggestively?—
sexually?

No.

Did he ever speak to you in such a way as to
suggest—

I've been telling you, no.

He did ask you to speak with him after class, Darren?

. . . Maybe, yeah. But just about . . .

About what, Darren?

Schoolwork. One of the class assignments.

How many times did he make this request, Darren?

. . .

Is that a refusal to answer, or don't you remember?

I guess it might've been once or twice. . . .

You met with your English teacher Lowell Tracy after school, in his office, once or twice last semester . . .

No. Just, like, in the classroom. After class.

But not after school? Just after class?

. . . I told you.

At these times when you were alone with Lowell Tracy . . .

We weren't alone! The door was open; people

were going out, coming in for the next class. There were lots of people around.

Would you define these meetings as student-teacher conferences?

I guess so. Sure.

At these times Lowell Tracy did not speak to you suggestively?

I told you, no.

He did not speak to you sexually?

No!

He did not touch you suggestively or sexually?

No.

But he did touch you, Darren, didn't he? Yes?

No, he did not. No!

He gave no hint of . . . made no gesture that might be interpreted as . . . inappropriate between a schoolteacher and his sixteen-year-old student, in the months you've known him?

I keep telling you, no.

Yet other boys have come forward to suggest otherwise. And some of these boys are your friends, Darren?

I don't know.

Don't know—what? That the boys are your friends, or—?

Just don't know! Anything about it.

Not anything, Darren?

No!

[3/18 interview abruptly discontinued. Interviewee agitated.]

[3/19 interview]

Darren, you've said that Lowell Tracy never invited you to his home in North Falls? Do you know where his home is?

No.

He never invited you to his home.

No! He didn't.

Did he speak of his home, of what might be there, food, drugs, liquor, videos, "games," in a way to make you want to visit him?

No. Definitely not.

Did he offer you gifts, Darren? Money?

No!

You seem surprised, Darren. Or upset?

Yeah . . . I guess I am.

That Lowell Tracy has been accused of offering gifts and money to a number of boys, this surprises you? Upsets you? Or that your name has been linked with his?

[Pause] My name is . . . linked with his?

You're certain you never went with Lowell Tracy to his house?

I told you no. I mean, yes, I'm certain.

You did not.

I did not.

He did not show you pornographic materials? Magazines, videos? In his home, or elsewhere?

No!

Yet you accompanied Lowell Tracy in his car, Darren? Did you?

No.

You did not accompany Lowell Tracy in his car? Ever?

No!

But you did accompany Lowell Tracy in his car, Darren, didn't you? At least once? Or more than once?

I keep telling you, no. [Pause] I guess I don't want to talk anymore.

You were never in Lowell Tracy's car?

No.

Never alone in Lowell Tracy's company, away from school, in his car?

. . . No.

You don't seem certain, Darren.

. . .

Maybe he gave you a ride home from school? How many times?

. . .

Darren, what would you say if I told you that you were identified as having been in the company of Lowell Tracy, last November, alone with him in his car?

Who . . . said that?

Is it true, Darren?

No. . . .

The mother of one of your classmates at North Falls identifies you as the boy who was with Lowell Tracy in his car outside the Coffee Cowboy sometime in late November 2003. She claims that she met Lowell Tracy inside the coffee shop, tried to engage him in conversation, but he was "sort of agitated, nervous—not friendly like he usually is."

Tracy left the coffee shop, and she left soon after and happened to see him in his car parked nearby, and—"Definitely, it was Darren Flynn with him—I was surprised at the time but never told anyone, I guess. Thinking, well—

I don't know what I was thinking. I guess I'm not a suspicious person."

Darren, what do you say to that?

. . .

Darren, there is nothing to be ashamed of. If Lowell Tracy forced himself on you, took advantage of his position to harass or proposition or exploit you, it is not your fault, Darren. Just tell us the truth. This interview is absolutely confidential and no names will be made public, and even should there be a criminal trial, the names of minors who have testified against Lowell Tracy will be kept strictly—

[Interviewee leaves room abruptly; interview discontinued]

47

Tell the truth. Tell what you know.
  Follow your conscience. Never lie!
  Stand up for your rights.
  And don't—ever!—be a snitch.

When Darren was ten, in fifth grade, his father took him out to McDonald's for a treat. Just Darren and Dad.

The occasion was a Talk with Dad. But it was a good talk, the best of all Talks with Dad.

This was a time when Darren was of only average height for his age, and underweight. His face was fine boned, rather girlish. His eyes filled easily with tears. In another two years he would grow to be one of the tallest boys in his class, one of the best athletes, but not just yet. Often he came home from school crying; older boys liked to push him around and taunt him:

"*Dar*-ren! Dar-ren!" He'd been ashamed, hadn't wanted his mother to tell his father, but of course she had.

Walt told Darren to stand up for his rights. Never run away, never cry. "It's only cowards who pick on smaller kids. They want you to run and cry, but you won't. I'll show you how."

They went back to the house, and Walt gave Darren his first boxing lesson.

It was thrilling for the ten-year-old to be taught to hold his fists like a boxer, how to crouch to protect his face and body. How to jab with his left hand, fast-fast. Fast! In this way you confuse and distract your opponent while with your right, your stronger arm, you hit. "As hard as you can. While you can."

Dad was patient with him, trying not to laugh when Darren flailed at him with shut eyes. They didn't use boxing gloves; the lessons were never so formal. What mattered was the strategy, the attitude. "Hit fast and furious, Darren. Swarm all over your opponent; don't give him a chance to hit back." Walt told him to behave as if he were a little crazy and not scared. He taught him that even if he was hit, and hurt, not to tell his teachers: "You don't want a reputation as a snitch. Believe me, that will only make things worse. If the situation is really bad, come to me. I'll take care of it."

But Darren hadn't needed to come to his father for help after these instructions. He'd learned to defend himself, and he'd liked the feeling.

Except now. Six years later. He hadn't a clue how to defend himself. Who was the enemy, even.

He'd tried to tell the detectives the truth, when he could. His strategy going into the interview had been to protect himself: not to defend Mr. Tracy but not to seem to be accusing him, either.

(Damn, he'd have liked to tell the detectives that Kevin Pyne and the others were lying to them!—but of course he couldn't. *Don't ever be a snitch*.)

(He'd have liked to tell the detectives that Mr. Tracy was a nice man who'd made a pass at him but had immediately retracted it and apologized, and was that a crime? Was it even a big deal? But of course he couldn't.)

It was stunning to Darren to be told that some-one had seen him in Mr. Tracy's car that afternoon. That single time, back in November! It was like a bad dream! The mother of a classmate coming out of the Coffee Cowboy at just that time. *Definitely, it was Darren Flynn with him—I was surprised at the time but never told anyone. . . .*

And would she now? Now that Mr. Tracy was under investigation, and there were rumors of sex crimes, perversion? Darren wondered who the woman was. How she could be so sure she'd seen him, and not some other boy? In the falling snow, through the messed-up windshield, Darren Flynn's face?

He'd panicked in the interview. The detectives had blindsided him. It was so; they'd been friendly, they'd seemed to like him and had treated him respectfully, even when he'd clammed up and made an asshole of himself. But they believed he was lying, they believed they had an eyewitness to refute his claim never to have been alone with Mr. Tracy in his car or anywhere else. . . . It was Detective Tyding who'd told Darren there was "nothing to be ashamed of," but this wasn't so; there was plenty to be ashamed of if you were a sixteen-year-old high school boy, a jock desperate not to be linked with a suspected "fag."

Darren Flynn, a name on the list.

"So, bro? How'd it go down at headquarters?"

Eddy's fist thumped him, a little too hard, on the shoulder.

Eddy was smiling at him, trying not to appear uneasy. Darren had to assume that Eddy had been hearing things about the investigation from his cop friend, and one of the things he'd been hearing was that Walt Flynn's younger son had been interviewed.

But the interview itself was confidential. Darren needed to believe that.

He told Eddy that things were OK. Things were fine.

"You done now? Or are they gonna call you back?"

"I'm done. I'm not going back."

Eddy hesitated. Eddy had more to say but looked as if he wasn't sure how to say it.

Hey, I know you're not queer, kid. I know you're not a fag.

You're my brother, bullshit you could be a fag.

48

Three days later Lowell Tracy was dead.

At 10:08 P.M. on March 22, Molly Rawlings called Darren to tell him the news she'd just heard from a friend of her mother's. Molly spoke so rapidly, at first Darren wasn't sure what she was saying.

". . . a car crash, just tonight! Not far from you, on Route Eleven! They're saying that Mr. Tracy was driving north out of town, hit a stretch of black ice and lost control of his car, skidded across the highway and crashed, about two hours ago it happened. Oh, Darren, isn't this terrible? Isn't this tragic? He died 'instantaneously,' they're saying, thank God for that. The poor man! He was so wonderful! I can't believe this, can you? It was around by the entrance to that old mall where the accident happened; it can't be more than a mile or so from your house; oh, Darren, maybe you heard the sirens—"

Darren hadn't, though. He was sure.

Darren sat on the edge of his bed, stunned. It would be one of the shocks of his life.

"Dead . . ."

The word was so blunt: *dead*.

Almost, you had to wonder what it meant. If it meant *gone*. If it meant *Won't ever see him again*.

If it meant *And you are to blame*.

By the time Molly hung up the phone, she'd begun crying. It was disconcerting to Darren to hear his friend so shaken, so emotional; he'd never heard Molly cry before, she was such an even-tempered and sunny-natured girl, one of the Good Christian Girls at NFH. Darren had wanted instinctively to comfort her as she wept. Saying, "Molly, come on, hey. Molly, don't cry . . ." as if Molly Rawlings were the stricken one, the distressing news, and not Mr. Tracy.

Darren felt numbed, unmoved. His face was

stiff as if with Novocain.

His mind was blank. An empty computer screen.

The Flynns were usually in bed by eleven P.M. weekdays. Though lately Eddy had been staying away overnight. (With his divorcée lover, Ruthie, a source of strained smiles and teary eyes on his mother's part.) In his room Darren sometimes stayed up later, but he needed sleep, at least eight hours. Tonight he went stealthily downstairs into the darkened family room to switch on the TV to watch the local eleven-P.M. news.

He kept the TV mute, crouched in front of the flickering screen.

Nothing about Lowell Tracy that night.

49

In the morning, all of North Falls knew.

By afternoon, there was a front-page news item in the *Lebanon Standard*, which everyone in North Falls read:

> **Lowell S. Tracy, 36, resident of North Falls and since 2001 an English and drama teacher at North Falls High School, died last night on Route 11 in a single-car accident. Police believe that Tracy's car lost control on an icy stretch of highway north of North Falls at about 9:45 p.m. A passing motorist called 911, but Tracy was pronounced dead at the scene by emergency medical workers.**
>
> **Tracy, currently on leave from his teaching position, was a native of Brookline, Massachusetts, and a 1988 summa cum laude graduate of Tufts University. He received master's degrees in English literature and public school education from Boston University.**
>
> **Corinth County issued a travelers' advisory last night as a combination of snow, sleet and low**

**temperatures made driving conditions hazardous
throughout the area.**

The photo of Lowell Tracy accompanying the
news item showed him without the trademark
little beard that gave him such a jaunty, self-con-
fident look. Tracy had more hair on his head, and
differently styled glasses, and was smiling somewhat quizzically at the camera like a man whose
name has just been called. Darren was shocked at
how young he looked.

Weird to think: Lowell Tracy had once been a
teenager. . . .

"So this is him. 'Tracy.'"

Walt Flynn's voice was flat, neutral. His fore-
finger stabbed at the smiling photo.

Darren exited the kitchen quickly, before his
father could say more.

50

On Route 11 north of town: why?

At nine forty-five P.M. on a Monday night: why?

In "hazardous" driving conditions: why?

At North Falls High it would be said that Mr. Tracy "totaled" his car.

Totaled was a guy word, uttered with awe and respect.

Totaled in a single-car accident was code for crashing at a high speed.

51

Girls were weeping openly. Most of the boys sat dry-eyed but subdued, respectful.

For the second time in a few weeks Mr. Newlove hastily called a special assembly to make an announcement concerning his "colleague" Lowell Tracy. This time Newlove appeared stricken, somewhat dazed. He stood behind the podium, squinting at notes: The funeral for Lowell Tracy would be private, in Brookline, Massachusetts, but there would be a memorial service here at school in May or June; he hoped that many of Mr. Tracy's students would wish to participate. . . .

There was a rumor that a small group of gay and lesbian students had organized at North Falls High, incensed by the "homophobic campaign" against Mr. Tracy. They were seniors, juniors, sophomores daring to come out in the hostile North Falls jock culture. Darren saw them sitting together in the first row of the auditorium. Had to hand it to them, they were brave. Six, seven guys and three girls.

He felt relief; they were no one he knew.

Darren was one of the somber, dry-eyed boys. Darren was one of the very quiet boys.

In the row ahead of Darren, Kevin Pyne several times glanced back at him, his eyes snatching at Darren's as if to say, *Not my fault! How's it my fault?* Darren ignored him.

The assembly was brief, less than fifteen minutes. Mr. Newlove had never appeared so shaken and uncertain. Several times he ceased speaking, simply staring at the notes in his wobbly hand as if he'd never seen them before. (Would Newlove break down and cry? A shiver of dread rippled through the audience. Nothing more awful, makes you cringe and want to hide your face, than an adult male breaking down, oh, man!) But Mr. Newlove got through the ordeal, to everyone's relief.

You were supposed to leave assembly quietly. Row
by row, in order. Darren Flynn had a way of easing out
ahead of others, like a fast-swimming fish among
slower, dumber fish. In three or four long strides he
was out of the auditorium and able to breathe.

"Hey, Darren—"

It was Barry Phelps, another fast-swimming fish.

"It's . . . sad, huh? It's a real surprise. . . ."

Barry shook his head, not knowing what to say.
Darren wasn't about to help him.

"You think it was, like, an actual . . . accident?
But why'd he'd be out there, huh? Why'd anybody
be out *there?*"

Darren swallowed hard. Darren walked away.

He'd avoid the guys. The guys would avoid him.
Except for swim team; he'd have to see them then, If
he stayed on the team.

Molly Rawlings was standing by her opened
locker, wiping at her eyes. The corridor was crowded;

people were moving to their first-period classes, which had been delayed by the assembly. Darren's first impulse was to avoid Molly; in her eyes that brimmed with emotion he was expected to be a better person than he was.

Seeing her so upset, though, made him feel a sudden rush of affection for her. He wanted to protect her! Went to comfort her, squeezing her arm, hugging her. "Hey. It's OK, Molly." In the corridor, classmates were regarding them with interest. It wasn't typical of Darren Flynn, who had a reputation for being aloof, to hang out at any girl's locker, let alone be so openly affectionate. Molly began to cry harder, her face crinkling in childish sorrow.

Something glinted around her neck: a silver heart locket that looked familiar to Darren.

". . . oh, Darren, why people turned against him I don't know! It happened so fast! . . . so cruel, so . . . hateful. We are meant to love and forgive one another, not to hate. The awful things people were saying about Mr. Tracy like it was a joke, and Mr. Tracy wasn't able to defend himself. . . . Now they're saying he did it on purpose, it wasn't an accident with his car, that would be even more tragic—I don't believe it! Mr. Tracy would never injure anyone, including himself. He had such a wonderful sense of humor! He was such a wonderful teacher! He loved North Falls High. He said so, lots of times. He was hard on us because he took us seriously, he said. He liked you, Darren, said he missed you in our class, your 'poise and presence. . . .' "

Darren held Molly, letting her cry. He was conscious of his hands on her back, the flesh of her upper back, and he was conscious of her hair, which was shiny and curly and of a fair-brown hue he would not have recalled if he'd shut his eyes. His face smarted as if he'd been slapped. Poise and presence!

So weird. It was all invented, wasn't it? People saw in others what they wanted to see, not what was there.

They saw, and fell in love with, what they saw. Not what was there.

Even as Molly wept, she was optimistic, hopeful. Making plans for the memorial service, she said she would ask to read a poem of Mr. Tracy's, and talk about what an "inspiring, awesome" teacher he'd been.

"Would you too, Darren? Say something about Mr. Tracy?"

"Sure."

Dry-eyed, though his eyes ached as if he'd been swimming in heavily chlorinated water.

52

Out of his e-mail trash Darren retrieved the message from *ltracy* he had not finished reading.

March 16, 2004

Dear Darren,

Forgive me, I promised I would not appeal to you again. But I have heard that you may be interviewed soon by North Falls detectives!

Please speak on my behalf, Darren. You need only tell the truth. I always respected and honored you. Perhaps I did "feel" for you something that was not welcomed by you, or understood by you, but I did not act upon this, Darren. (Did I?)

I know, I embarrassed you. But I embarrassed myself more.

As to why I am being persecuted here in North Falls, I have some suspicions. My high standards are a threat to certain students. There is a conspiracy against me to destroy me. It began at the end of last term. Perhaps I was blind. I was stubborn. My "high standards" in North Falls were a melancholy joke.

The investigating detectives repeat only that there are accusers against me who are minors; their names must be kept confidential. There is "evidence" of the most ludicrous kind, crude pornographic material that makes me sick just to look at.

Even my poetry has been used against me. Read aloud by an uncomprehending detective. If this situation were not so awful, I would find it the most hilarious farce.

I voluntarily and (my mistake) without a lawyer present agreed to be interviewed by North Falls detectives. Long, grueling sessions that left me exhausted, and the detectives more intent upon a confession. Of my volition I took a polygraph test twice. The first time, I was so nervous, the results were "inconclusive"; the second time, the results were negative, meaning that I passed.

Yet it seemed to make no difference to my persecutors. (Polygraph results aren't admissible in court, they said!)

If there is a public hearing, even if there is a

trial, my accusers can remain anonymous. I have pleaded with our cowardly principal to examine these accusers, but he refuses, he so fears lawsuits from angry parents.

And so I am being slandered and cannot defend myself. It has become the worst of nightmares!

There will be no public hearing. There will be no trial. I will not endure this public humiliation.

Darren, I appeal to you. But if you wish not to speak for me, I can understand. It's too much to ask of you, perhaps.

God be with you.

Sincerely,

Lowell Tracy

It was a warning, wasn't it? Like a suicide note.

No trial. I will not endure.

Darren read the message and reread it. He was disgusted with himself for not having read it earlier. When Lowell Tracy was still alive.

I should have helped him. Why didn't I help him . . . ?

He'd been a coward, that was why. Fearful of what others would say. Fearful of what his father would say.

And he couldn't have denounced his friends. He just couldn't.

He was a guy's guy, a jock. If he wasn't, what was he?

53

Next day there was a packet for Darren Flynn in the mail. A manila envelope with no return address, postmarked North Falls. Darren found it lying amid utility bills and advertising flyers on the kitchen table, where his mother had left it.

Darren never received mail. You couldn't blame Edith Flynn for being curious.

"Something for you, Darren. Wonder what it is. . . ."

His breath came short. Blindly, Darren snatched up the envelope and took it away with him to his room.

He opened the envelope with shaking fingers. His name and address were carefully hand-printed. He didn't know what the envelope contained, but he knew who it was from.

Photographs. Taken at school swim meets. Darren was astonished to see himself in every photo. Darren on the high board preparing to dive, Darren in mid dive, Darren in the agitated aqua water caught as he surfaced, gasping for air. Darren standing at the edge of the pool in just his purple Speedo trunks, frowning at someone (Coach?) out of camera range. There was Darren with his teammates, towels draped around their necks. And Darren in profile approaching the edge of the pool, a tall, lean boy with silvery-gold hair, long-legged, with a swimmer's broad shoulders and lean waist.

Darren shoved the photos away, disgusted.

He knew who'd taken them. Knew who'd sent them. There was no note inside the envelope, but he knew.

54

Darren stayed out of school for the rest of the week. He wasn't sick, he told his mother. Though he looked sick; his skin appeared feverish, and his eyes were reddened.

"Just I can't take it. 'Poor Mr. Tracy' blah blah blah. Hypocrite bullshit."

"Darren! What a way to talk."

Edith Flynn was shocked, her younger son so sullen and rude. And such an unexpected word to hear from him: *hypocrite*.

He smelled angry. He hadn't shaved for several days. His jaws were covered in pale glinting hairs like separate wires. His eyes were faintly bloodshot, as if he'd been swimming, though he hadn't.

Edith put out a hand to touch Darren, gently. He flinched and shook it off.

"Maybe you are sick, Darren. You certainly aren't yourself."

Darren laughed, in that way he'd always had of deflecting her annoyance with him. "Who am I then, Mom? Mike Tyson?"

In boots and hooded waterproof jacket, he hiked through back fields, avoiding Route 11. It was about a mile to the river, where there were graveled hiking trails, rutted and all but impassable in snow.

The river was the Connecticut, frozen over since November and covered in layers of rippled snow.

It was late March, but very cold. The air was still, but cold. Since Darren had last hiked along the river, the sun had shifted conspicuously in the sky. You could tell the season was late winter, nearing spring.

Hiking, he'd worked up a sweat. Something like an oily tear ran down his cheek. He climbed an embankment to an old iron bridge that crossed the river beside a railroad bridge. In warm weather the water below ran swiftly and appeared black; in winter the water was hidden beneath snow. You had to imagine that treacherous black water rushing invisibly beneath.

Darren leaned on the railing, staring down. He was so tired!

Traffic passed behind him, sporadically. The old bridge creaked.

. . . speak on my behalf, Darren. . . . only tell the truth.

He hadn't. He hadn't said enough to the detectives. Hadn't even tried.

Everything he'd said had sounded wrong. Like a lie. Even the truth sounded like a lie. The way the detectives had pursued him, he'd panicked and run. There was no way for him to explain about Mr. Tracy, nor had he adequate words. He wasn't a boy for whom words came easily; he was like a novice swimmer tossed into choppy water. Swim or sink.

Swim desperately, or sink.

He hadn't been brave enough, either. He would have to live with that.

Mr. Tracy knew, probably. That Darren was such a coward. He'd forgiven him, even. *God be with you.*

"Sure. He knew."

It wasn't enough just to rip the photos into pieces. Darren had to burn them too.

Back in a field behind the garage. Where no one would ever discover the evidence. A thrill of horror came over him at the prospect of his father, or Eddy, seeing the photos. Darren would rather die, he thought.

It was disgusting, seeing himself through Lowell Tracy's eyes. Seeing himself *that way*. Darren in the tight-fitting Speedo trunks. His crotch, loins. His flat, hard-muscled stomach and navel.

Not me. None of that is me.

It was weird, Darren didn't identify with the

boy in the photos. There were shots of that person, you'd think he was as old as nineteen, twenty. You wouldn't think he was a kid. You wouldn't think he had rashlike pimples at his hairline and across his shoulders, which Coach said were caused by nerves. You wouldn't think his heart was pounding inside his taut-muscled chest and there was a sick terror in his gut that he would fuck up. He looked confident, smiling and assured with his buddies; even on the high board his expression seemed calm, imperturbed. It was Darren Flynn's public face, he guessed. You had to hide so much.

"Bullshit."

When Darren arrived back at the house, there was his mother just climbing into her car in the driveway. She waved, and waited for him.

Almost, for a sickening moment, he forgot he'd destroyed the photos of himself and thought his mother had found them.

"Darren, it's so cold to be hiking. Is that what

you were doing—hiking? When you're feverish, and exhausted?"

Darren mumbled a reply, brushing hair out of his eyes.

"I'm worried about you, honey. You've stayed out of school, which isn't like you, and you're been so remote and not yourself. . . . It doesn't have anything to do, does it"—Edith Flynn blinked and swallowed, forcing a smile—"with this incident at school? I mean, obviously it does, it must, that man, and the police questioning you . . ."

Darren mumbled a reply, wiping at his nose.

"I wish you'd talk to me, honey. I know, with your father it can be a little awkward sometimes, but I hope you know you can talk with me."

"Sure, Mom."

Darren tried to smile, to assure her. His mother was anxious, and he loved her.

Later he would realize that his mother had meant to drive out looking for him. She'd come back into the house with him; there could be no other explanation.

Looking for him, in her car! As if she'd have been able to find him, if he'd wanted to disappear.

55

The meet with St. John's was next week.

Darren missed practice twice. Swam by himself in the pool so charged up he wanted never to stop. In his head imagining not the St. John's swimmers but Olympic swimmers and he was swimming to qualify for the Olympics; swim your heart out, Darren, swim your heart out in the four-hundred-meter freestyle you will lose—you're fated to lose, but the crowd will love you. Just a high school kid from New Hampshire, an obscure small-town school no one has ever heard of, though you have a terrific coach, but he's no one famous, nor has there ever been anyone remotely famous associated with North Falls, New Hampshire.

Swim your heart out! What else do you have?

His strokes were coming ragged. His breathing

was off. Hairs sprouting on his body that he'd have to shave before the St. John's meet if he swam with the team, which maybe he would not, coarse hairs on his chest, his legs, his forearms, and the hair on his head overlong, sloppy. What he admires in skilled swimmers is their keeping their rhythm through a race, not allowing the competition to throw them off stride, and the ease with which they turn, flip and move underwater and surface again in virtually the same moment; he's executed the moves a thousand times but always has to worry he'll crash his head against the concrete, split his skull and spill his brains. *Fuckup Dar-ren!* He hasn't been diving lately. He can't bear it, climbing up onto the diving board, exposing himself. Swimming he can do, swimming is not exposure, you can actually hide in the water, but he'd lost count of the laps, he was confused now, his vision blotched and he was only just swimming because (this was crazy! but it was so) he'd forgotten how to stop. One arm and then the other, and his feet kicking. Half sobbing now; his breath burned his lungs. His heart was thudding. The chlorine smell was really getting to him like (maybe) snorting heroin might when Coach came running out, to yell in a booming voice Darren hadn't ever heard from him before, "Are you crazy, Flynn? Get out of that pool before you kill yourself."

56

That weekend Molly called.

Her voice was hushed, excited: "Darren, can you drop by the house this afternoon? I've got a surprise to show you."

Surprise to show you. Molly sounded like a little girl, thrilled.

The mood Darren was in, it was something of a shock to hear from a friend in so different a mood. He was feeling as if, if he spat out saliva, it would look ashy.

When he'd missed two days of school that week, Molly had e-mailed him—twice—to ask if something was wrong. Darren hadn't replied.

On his way to town, Eddy dropped Darren off at the Rawlingses' house. Big white colonial on Church Street with dark shutters and a red front door, bronze eagle knocker on the door. In the driveway was Mrs. Rawlings's Mercedes-Benz and Mr. Rawlings's Land Rover and one of those sporty little Volkswagens belonging to Molly's college-age brother. Eddy whistled through his teeth as if impressed.

"Here y'are, bro. Don't forget to wipe your feet."

Darren laughed. He supposed it was funny.

Molly was waiting just inside the door in the vestibule. As Darren came up the flagstone walk, she opened the door and called out happily, "Darren, look who I have! This is Pandora."

Squirming in Molly's arms was a small taffy-colored spaniel with wet-looking black eyes.

"Mr. Tracy's dog. She's come to live with us."

Molly spoke breathlessly. Almost, there was an air of defiance in her voice.

Mr. Tracy's dog! Darren heard himself say he hadn't known that Mr. Tracy had a dog. . . .

(He'd known. In his car, Mr. Tracy had said something about dog hairs on the seat.)

Molly was the happiest Darren had seen her in a

while. Her hair was tied back in a ponytail; she wore a turtleneck sweater and the gleaming silver locket around her neck. She invited Darren into the Rawlingses' sprawling family room, where close by the fireplace she'd fixed Pandora's bed, a cushioned wicker basket. The dog was the smallest spaniel Darren had ever seen,

". . . Mr. Tracy's downstairs neighbor he'd been really friendly with, this woman who's on some committee with my mom, she was telling us how Mr. Tracy went out that night, leaving Pandora with her, saying he'd be out of town for a few days and couldn't take Pandora with him, and this friend of my mom's really wanted to keep Pandora, but it isn't practical for her, and Mr. Tracy's parents are like too old for a dog, or allergic, and so . . . Pandora is living with us now, aren't you?" Molly laughed as the little curly-haired dog lunged to lick and kiss at her face.

Pandora was nearly as friendly with Darren. She rushed at him to lick effusively at his hands; her hindquarters shimmied in excitement. "Hey! You're a real love bug, aren't you?" Darren laughed; the little dog had won his heart.

The Flynns had had a dog for nine years, a mixed-breed shepherd. When he'd died a few years before, the loss had been so painful, Darren's mother said, "Never again!"

Molly said earnestly, "Pandora was desperate missing Mr. Tracy, whimpering and whining, and couldn't stay still until just this morning; she's calming down a little. She has to know that her new family won't abandon her. If dogs could understand! I could try to explain that Mr. Tracy went away somewhere and couldn't take her with him. I could make her know that he loves her and misses her, but he just isn't here."

Darren was squatting; the little spaniel lunged and squirmed in his arms. He pressed his face against her, into her curly-furred neck. Damn if he would let Molly see him cry. Bit his lower lip, hard. The weak moment passed.

Molly lowered her voice as if not wanting

Pandora to hear. She touched Darren's wrist; the hairs stirred on his arm.

Eddy said if a girl or a woman touches you, it means she wants you to touch her back.

"The funeral was yesterday. Nobody from North Falls went, I guess."

Funeral. For a confused moment Darren didn't know what Molly meant.

"Just Mr. Tracy's relatives and old, close friends. If he had any friends here, I guess his relatives in Brookline didn't want them."

"Well. You can't blame them."

"Oh, I don't know! It wasn't Mr. Tracy's friends who said such things about him."

Molly's eyes brimmed with quick emotion. She was one who seemed not to understand, or to wish to understand, that even friends could betray you. Not by anything they did but by what they failed to do.

Darren squeezed Molly's hand; her fingers closed about his. She was eager, hopeful, affectionate as the squirmy little taffy-colored spaniel. With a pang of guilt Darren thought what a generous person Molly was. Better than he deserved as a friend. He wanted to love her; maybe he could love her. Maybe what he already felt for Molly Rawlings was love.

57

Last summer Darren had followed the USA Swimming National Championships in College Park, Maryland. A young man named Michael Phelps had emerged as the star. He'd won five of fourteen individual titles for men, the first swimmer in history to win five men's events at one national competition. And this after winning four gold medals at the World Swimming Competition in Barcelona, Spain.

In College Park, Phelps had set a world record in the two-hundred-meter individual medley. His time was 1 minute 55.96 seconds.

Darren read and reread these statistics. Not wanting to think what his own best swim time for two hundred meters was.

Coach said not to be comparing yourself with guys like Phelps except as an example of what can happen if you take swimming seriously, if you really train.

Darren laughed. If you take swimming seriously! If you really train!

Phelps swam butterfly, backstroke, freestyle. Phelps was said to have "weaknesses," which meant he had room to grow.

On a window ledge by his computer table, Darren had taped a newspaper clipping of rawboned, big-eared, smiling Phelps displaying his gold and silver medals. A guy's guy, you could tell. He looked a little like Jimmy Kovaks.

Darren had memorized Phelps's remarks:

> **I like pressure. It helps me get fired up.**
> **I hate failing. I hate losing. I love to compete in sport. I love to race. I want to break as many records as possible. I want to swim my fastest every race.**
> **I just try to be a normal person. I don't think it's hard. But the things I do now, not everyone my age is doing.**

Phelps had just turned eighteen.

58

They were partially blocking the sidewalk behind the school, which was bordered with jagged crusts of snow. People had to pass close around them, unnoticed by the boys. Strange to see two jocks talking together earnestly and not laughing and one of them in the other's face.

". . . like, nobody wanted him to die, Darren! It was just, stuff got out of control."

"Then say so. Tell Newlove. It should come out, what you guys did."

"It wasn't 'you guys'! It was Kevin and Drake mostly. That fucker Drake! He had the idea to send this shit to the police. We wouldn't have, except for him."

"What shit?"

Jimmy Kovaks shrugged. His gawky-boy face

looked pained. He was trying not to meet Darren's eye, though Darren stood in front of him.

Jimmy said evasively, "I don't know! I didn't see it, exactly. I mean, I saw the gay porn shit they pushed under Newlove's door, but I didn't see what they wrote on it. Darren, it was a joke! Some sick joke like on cable TV; we were laughing like hell. Anybody with half a brain could tell it was made-up shit, not real."

"This was something you sent to the police? What was it?"

"I don't know, I said! I didn't have that much to do with it. The stuff they put under Newlove's door, I saw that, I guess. It was this gay porn shit they took from some crappy magazines. The other stuff they sent to the police, I didn't." Jimmy paused. His breath was steaming. He had the look of a swimmer in the final desperate lap of a race when he's falling behind.

"The thing is, Darren, nobody wanted Tracy to die. I was pissed at him, but I didn't actually hate him. Kevin hated him, I guess, and Drake, why I don't know, Tracy never failed them, did he? Drake never even took a class with him. He's going around saying Tracy came on to him like he's bragging about it, but it's made up. You ask him, he says it's true. It's like him and Kevin kind of believe this stuff is true, now."

A bell was ringing inside school. Neither Jimmy nor Darren seemed to hear. Jimmy said, lowering his voice, "Man, you don't fool around with cops! It's like these airport security guys. You make a joke about a bomb on an airplane, you're fucked. They strip-search you, they interrogate you, the FBI arrests you. The cops are like that. Right here in North Falls, they're all over you right away. Soon as they got this stuff Kevin and Drake sent them, saying it was from some eleven-year-old kid who'd gotten mixed up with Tracy, they moved in on Tracy and Newlove both; they came to school here, and Newlove caved in like in five minutes. We're thinking it was Newlove who gave the cops the list, guys' names.

Kevin says he didn't give up anybody's name, but man! Maybe he did. He told Newlove that Tracy came on to guys, mostly athletes, saying he'd give them high grades if, like, they hooked up with him. Or if they didn't, he'd fail them."

Darren said, disgusted, "But you should have said something, Jimmy. When the detectives talked to you."

"My dad was right there! I couldn't."

"What do you mean, you couldn't? It's got to be against the law to lie to the police. Trying to ruin somebody's life, like a teacher's career, and not say anything when you could; it's hard to believe you'd do something like that, Jimmy! Kevin's mean hearted, Drake's some kind of psycho, but you . . ."

Jimmy protested, "I didn't know where it was headed, Darren. How'd anybody know? We're fooling around, anybody could figure out it was a joke, except cops exaggerate things, and the DA's office, these 'sex crimes' people, if it's anybody's fault, it's their fault, wanting to believe this shit about Tracy.

They didn't ever arrest him, I guess. But whatever he told them, it must've made everything worse. You know how he acted, kind of smart-ass. A guy like that, you'd never think . . ." Jimmy paused, looking pained. "I'm sorry now, Darren. I really am."

"So say something, Jimmy. You could."

Jimmy shook his head miserably. "Darren, you know I can't. And you can't either. Anything I said, or you said, the other guys would deny it; it's their word against ours. We can't snitch on our friends, we just can't. The cops and the DA people made up their minds right away, and they won't change their minds; they'd see Tracy killing himself like it's an admission of guilt. That's how they think. My dad thinks that. Mr. Tracy is dead, Darren, but we got to live here."

Darren looked around to see that he and Jimmy were alone, suddenly. The parking lot and the sidewalk were deserted. He'd forgotten where they were: behind North Falls High School. A buff-brick two-story building that wasn't old but looked weather-stained. A building like a factory, or a prison.

Inside, another bell was ringing.

"Man! We're gonna be late."

Jimmy ran to the door. Darren didn't follow.

He saw that it was a bright windy day. Still March, and still winter. Wet snow had fallen in the night, and there was a blinding icy glaze to things.

He decided not to enter the building just then. He would walk to the edge of the parking lot, along an access road behind the school, a mile or so to a railroad embankment, and there was the Connecticut River frozen and lifeless looking, and his nose was running and his eyes stung from the wind and he had to piss and he'd be in trouble at school, cutting more classes after staying out two days last week. He was alone, yet it was like Jimmy was still with him, pleading. Jimmy seemed more real to Darren than Darren did to himself. He'd known Jimmy Kovaks since junior high and they'd been friends but not close friends; now he felt—it was weird—he felt like

Jimmy was his brother, a brother closer to him than his own brother, Eddy, but why Darren was feeling this way, he didn't know. He was pissed at Jimmy, wasn't he?

You know I can't. And you can't either.

59

This scene! Like TV except clumsier and dumber and no laugh track to cue you it's meant to be funny.

Saying he wants to talk to Principal Newlove and the receptionist is looking at him startled and wary asking does he have an appointment with Mr. Newlove, isn't he a student and shouldn't he be in class, and if he isn't in class where is his official pink slip initialed by a teacher to allow him out of class between periods, and he smiles politely and repeats he wants to talk with Principal Newlove please taking care to enunciate these words *Princi-pal New-love* like they were a really big deal, like Newlove isn't an asshole and a pathetic coward not deserving of anybody's respect, by this time a second woman is on her feet approaching the waist-high Formica-topped counter behind which you aren't supposed to step uninvited and this woman is speaking to him in a voice sharper and more alarmed than the first, asking what is his name? what is his name? and the best strategy is deafness, he just walks past her headed for the closed door with the plaque JOHN L. NEWLOVE, PRINCIPAL and he's knocking and there's a voice inside and he's opening the door without waiting to be asked inside, the women are really agitated now like guinea hens clucking and fussing and there's the principal himself Mr. John L. Newlove, rising from his desk, gaping at Darren Flynn like Darren is a cyborg avenger or worse yet a Columbine psycho armed with a bazooka to blow Principal Newlove away so quickly he lifts his hands, extends his palms to show he is totally unarmed, totally harmless, only wants to ask Principal Newlove some questions, and Principal Newlove is stammering this isn't the time, this is not a good time, and Darren says yes it's a good time, it is a good time he thinks, Mr. Tracy has been dead for a week now, and Newlove is quivery mouthed, stammering he can't speak to Darren about Mr. Tracy, he is very sorry but absolutely he cannot, or about any police investigation, he is following the advice of legal counsel in refusing to speak on this subject, and Darren explains this is important, he has something important to say about Mr. Tracy, and Newlove is staring at him, then lunges suddenly to shut his office door in the faces of the excitable, aghast women, doesn't want the women to overhear, Newlove is telling Darren he cannot breach confidentiality, he cannot and will not, he is very sorry, and Darren is saying it's about the accusations against Mr. Tracy, they were not true they were lies they were made by students who wanted revenge, and Newlove presses his hands over his ears looking pained, half shutting his eyes saying no! no! I cannot discuss this matter, you must leave my office now, Darren Flynn, immediately you must leave or I will call security, I will call nine one one, and Darren says but don't you care, Mr. Newlove, Mr. Tracy is *dead*? he's, like, *dead*? and Newlove shakes his head as if not hearing, shakes his head so vehemently his jowls quiver; Darren sees the man is drawn with fatigue, sunken eyes and smudged-looking bifocals, his no-color hair has flipped the wrong way revealing a swath of sweaty scalp; half begging now, Newlove is saying I can't! I can't! and won't! this is a nightmare I must insist that you leave immediately, Darren Flynn, you are a good boy, a good student and a good citizen of our school community, you have always been a popular boy here, and a first-rate athlete, you should be proud of that, Darren, so many boys hope to be athletes of your caliber and so few succeed, I am willing to overlook this breach of conduct but you must leave, otherwise you will be suspended from school, you will be expelled from North Falls High, this aberrant behavior will be noted on your academic record, you will be admitted to no college or university, your entire academic future will be forfeit, Darren Flynn, do you hear? do you comprehend? or shall I call your parents? shall I place a call to your parents? would you like that, son, a distress call placed to your innocent parents? would you like them involved as well? would you like them upset as well? or will you leave my office immediately, and try to forget, as I will, that this unfortunate incident ever transpired, this tragic misunderstanding ever transpired? I am pleading with you, Darren Flynn, to listen to reason. . . .

And Darren sees it's hopeless, suddenly.

Sure. Hopeless. Should've known.

Darren has been swimming the limit of his strength blindly and desperately headed for the concrete wall of the pool, where he'll flip and make his turn and almost—almost!—he miscalculates and cracks his head, spilling his brains into the water, except Darren Flynn is in better control of the situation than you might think, he's smarter and shrewder than you think, and like that it's over.

"OK, Mr. Newlove. Sorry."

Newlove is gaping at him like he can't believe what he hears. Panting like somebody trapped on a treadmill turned to full speed. Poor old guy, looking like he's about to have a heart attack.

"You—you understand, Darren? I hope you—"

Darren laughs. "Sure."

60

Morning of the swim meet with St. John's, Wednesday, March 31.

Still, Darren isn't decided. Though that anxious feeling, built up and ready to discharge, means he's priming himself.

After third-period chemistry lab, waiting until the classroom was empty, needing to ask Mr. Labrador in an earnest voice *Is brain chemistry the same as the soul?* and when Mr. Labrador laughed at the question, he was hurt, asking *why's it funny, Mr. Labrador?* and Mr. Labrador (who would recount the incident later in the teachers' lounge, where his colleagues would shake their heads over what-was-happening-to-Darren-Flynn) said quickly *it isn't funny it's a perfectly legitimate question but requires a complex answer and now isn't the time to address it,* fourth period is coming up, so perhaps another time, Darren, all right?

Darren shrugs and slouches away.

Sure.

61

"Last kid I'd expect to perform like that," Coach Ellroy was reported to be saying of Darren Flynn even after Darren had astonished onlookers by swimming like a maniac at the meet with St. John's, coming in first in three events, including the four-hundred-meter freestyle. Even after Darren's performance secured the unexpected win (by two points) over St. John's and gave North Falls High something to celebrate.

Darren Flynn! He'd come up from behind, for all three wins. At the end of the four-hundred-meter, he'd been so exhausted, he had nearly crawled out of the pool, had to be helped by two teammates to make his way to the bench as the crowd cheered.

All that week the rumor was that Darren Flynn wouldn't be participating in the meet at all. He'd been cutting classes, staying out of school with no medical excuse. He'd missed swim practices. Coach was upset, and Coach was worried. Had to be pragmatic, pulling Darren from the scheduled diving events against St. John's, figuring it was too risky for everyone concerned to let the boy compete with St. John's superior divers.

But Darren might be OK for swimming, Coach decided. With Jimmy Kovaks off the team and everyone demoralized, Coach needed every warm body he could get his hands on, and the worst Darren could do was come in last, and somebody had to come in last, right? It's the nature of the game. You have to have losers if you're gonna have winners; it's the nature of the game of life. Right?

Coach was in a philosophical mood. Meaning he expected to lose, and to lose bad. Philosophy is for losers; if you're a winner, you don't have time for bullshitting.

Still, Coach nearly freaked before the meet when Darren finally showed up. The last of the twelve to arrive at poolside.

Darren hadn't shaved his body like the others. Hadn't as much body hair as some of the more developed boys, so he figured (he said, shrugging) his swim time wouldn't be that much affected. But what was making everyone stare was Darren hadn't had his hair cut, either; he'd tied it back in a tiny two-inch pigtail at the nape of his neck.

"What's that, Flynn? Pimp-style hair?"

It was meant as a joke. Or maybe not entirely a joke.

Darren seemed not to hear. He was clenching and unclenching his fists. Coach saw that the boy was breathing quickly and shallowly, and he hoped to hell some sort of berserk breakdown scene wasn't coming up in this public space.

This season, the St. John's team was leading the district. They had beaten every rival, including last year's champs, Lebanon High. The NFH team was intimidated by them. Their lead swimmer had beaten Jimmy Kovaks the previous year. They had two top divers, who were really good. At the meet you could see the St. John's boys strutting. They thought well of themselves. Many in the crowd had driven down from St. John's, a mill town on the Connecticut River fifteen miles to the north, to support them vociferously. In the opening events, one-hundred- and two-hundred-meter individual medleys, the St. John's team outswam NFH. In the two-hundred-meter backstroke, NFH—led by Darren Flynn, who'd never competed in a backstroke event before—outswam St. John's. Here was an upset; Coach was incredulous. Ten minutes later, Darren finished first in the three-hundred-meter freestyle, another upset. But Darren swam most impressively in the four-hundred-meter, coming up out of fourth place to overtake the other swimmers after he'd had a disappointing start—he'd looked winded, had not executed his first turn very gracefully, but then he was swimming with sudden frenzied swiftness, in the final lap steadily gaining and overtaking the lead St. John's swimmer, as the crowd stood screaming. In his body and at the same time out of it, hovering above it amid the deafening cries, *Swim your heart out! swim your heart out!* he could hear a man's voice, his English teacher's voice it was, and he could feel Mr. Tracy's touch on his lunging shoulders, his blessing, *God be with you.*

He hadn't seemed to realize the race was over. He was being helped out of the pool. His legs had dissolved. His vision had gone blotchy. There were shimmering halos around the ceiling lights. There was a clanging in his ears; you'd think the school alarm system had gone off. Would've slipped in a puddle of water if Ross Slaugh hadn't grabbed him. His mother, whom he had not allowed to touch him for two weeks, was hugging him, not minding how wet he was. His father was crushing him in a big bear hug. There was Eddy, laughing and pounding on him. All the guys, guys' faces transformed in triumph. Even Kevin, who hated his guts. And Coach, shaking his big-domed head, astonished. Coach, who'd be in shock for days, if not for the rest of the season.

Trying to catch his breath. The danger was hyperventilating. His heart was still thudding. The crowd was still noisy. He saw Molly Rawlings waving to him. Molly Rawlings with a proud, shining face. The sports reporter for the *Lebanon Standard* was interviewing him, asking aggressively how's it feel, Darren Flynn? how's it feel to be underdog who comes out on top? and Darren was saying, raising his voice to be heard over the din: "The team was swimming tonight in memory of our teacher Mr. Tracy, who died in a car crash on March 22. Our victory tonight is in his honor. Mr. Tracy really"—Darren swiped at his eyes, which were bloodshot and raw-looking from the water—"really supported the team."

It would appear next day on the front page of the *Lebanon Standard*:

SPECTACULAR NFH SWIM TEAM VICTORY
IN MEMORY OF POPULAR ENGLISH TEACHER

62

It was Easter break. It was April, a new season. The ice crust had melted from the Connecticut River as if it had never been, and now the water ran swift and dark and treacherous between the muddy, overgrown banks. Darren had a new routine of hiking along the river, sometimes for as long as two hours. It was a time for clearing his head, thinking seriously about the future. What his dad expected of him, how he'd get along with the guys, whether he wanted to stay on the team . . . After the meet with St. John's, Darren Flynn had become a local hero, approached by strangers in stores and on the street who wanted to shake his hand and thank him, even some younger kids who asked for his autograph! He liked the attention but guessed it wouldn't last. The way people would begin to forget Mr. Tracy and how he'd been treated . . . After Darren's performance against St. John's, when Coach Ellroy had recovered enough from his shock to resume his old sense of humor, he'd said to Darren, "Now you'll have to outdo your record, Flynn." It was a new, kind of scary thought.

"But I don't have to. Not if I don't want to. I can quit the team. I'm not a slave to the team. I can . . ."

Darren hiked faster, working up a sweat. What he loved was feeling his heart beat just a little hard, a plunging sensation in his blood, a sense of not knowing what the hell he would do, and whose business was it, except Darren Flynn's?

63

Phone rings, and it's a low, throaty, sulky-sexy almost-familiar voice: "Remember me, Darren? Jill Brockmeier."

Darren is so taken by surprise, all he can do is mumble, "Sure!"

It's spring break at the colleges. All this week are impromptu parties given by college students back in town and eager to see their friends and former classmates, and to some of these parties the more popular—"high-profile"—North Falls High students are being invited.

As if *Darren Flynn* were a name on a mysterious list.

"So, Darren! I've been hearing some really terrific, awesome things about you. The swim meet with what's it, Lebanon High . . ."

"St. John's."

"Right! You were really, really fantastic, everybody is saying. Anyway . . ."

Jill has called to invite Darren to a party the following evening, any time after nine P.M. It's looking to be a really big party, Jill says. A terrific party. Jill hopes he can come.

Darren is vague. Darren isn't sure. Well, maybe. Darren asks if he can bring someone.

"Who?"

It's an almost-rude question. Darren guesses he has offended Jill Brockmeier.

"A friend from school, Molly Rawlings . . ."

There is another pause. Darren can almost see Jill Brockmeier screwing up her face. He seems to recall it's a very attractive face unless, somehow, he's confusing it with the face of the female detective Tyding.

Tyding! She and Forrester had really fucked Darren Flynn up, backing him into a corner he couldn't get out of. They must have known he was lying to them, but nothing had come of it anyway.

After Mr. Tracy died, nothing had come of any of it, like a bad dream you're miserable thinking is real but as soon as you wake, you begin to forget and soon afterward have a hard time remembering why you'd been so miserable trapped inside it.

"Sure, Darren. If you want."

Jill goes on to tell Darren that she's a sophomore at the U of New Hampshire at Durham; she pledged Chi Omega and is undecided between a major in business administration and "environment." She tells Darren that she loves UNH, but she misses her old high school friends a lot. She'd been hearing some "really cool, exciting things" about Darren. She asks again, with a little dip to her voice, if he remembers her: She'd gone out with Emory Slaugh their senior year at NFH. She'd been a varsity cheerleader.

Darren is remembering Jill Brockmeier now, vaguely. He hasn't seen or thought of her in two years and doesn't know what to make of her calling him like this.

Jill gives Darren her address: 82 Holland Drive,

overlooking the Valley Golf and Country Club. Darren has never been out on Holland Drive; he has never been at the country club, though Molly Rawlings, whose parents are members, has invited him once or twice. He does know that the Brockmeiers are a prominent North Falls family. When he tells his mother where he's going, she will look at him startled. The Brockmeiers!

After he hangs up, Darren remembers Jill Brockmeier, a cheerleader who came on to him his sophomore year. Maybe she'd been joking or maybe she'd been serious, Darren never knew. He'd been intimidated by the older girl's sexual aggressiveness. He'd been intimidated by most girls, even those his own age.

His friends had been impressed. And envious.

Kevin had teased him: "Brockmeier's hot for you, Darren. Go for it."

He hadn't, though. Not Darren Flynn.

64

"Darren Flynn? H'*lo*."

A blond girl with mascara-widened neon eyes, must be Jill Brockmeier, throws open the massive door to her house, which is brightly lighted and emitting high decibels of sound like a manic pulse, pulls Darren into the vestibule and rises on her (bare) toes to brush his cheek with startlingly cool lips. Darren is unnerved by the gesture; he's rarely kissed on the cheek by anyone except female relatives.

"Ross! Ki-Ki! H'*lo*. Terrific to see you."

Darren wouldn't recognize Jill, maybe. Her hair is cropped short, bleached ash blond like the Madonna of years ago. But her eyebrows are darkish brown, and her mouth is some weird dark purple, smeared from where she's been kissing people, and drinking from a bottle of Coors Light. Though it's a chilly April night, Jill is wearing a glittery see-through tank top and no bra beneath, tight designer jeans with glittery studs. Her toenails have been painted blue to match her fingernails. On each of her fingers she wears an oversized ring. Darren is practically slack-jawed gaping at her, and Ross pokes him in the ribs, laughing. "C'mon, let's get drinks."

Darren has come to the party with Ross Slaugh and a girl named Ki-Ki, a senior at NFH. He decided not to ask Molly Rawlings, figuring the party won't be Molly's kind of party; she'd be out of place and want to go home. And Darren was thinking . . .

But Jill Brockmeier seems to have forgotten him. A crowd of guys is arriving, older guys Darren doesn't know, and Jill is squealing and greeting them with hugs and kisses like a little girl at Christmas. One of these guys kisses Jill full on the lips and grabs at her squirmy little ass.

Darren follows Ross into another room, a step-down family-type room thunderous with sound. It's only nine twenty P.M., and already there are maybe fifty people crowded into this room, and their ghost reflections in a wall of plate glass windows overlooking a terrace. On a stone ledge running the width of the room, beneath the largest digital TV screen Darren has ever seen, there's a tub of beer on ice. The tile floor in the vicinity of the tub is puddled with water.

He's underage, it's against state law for a minor to drink "alcoholic beverages," but Darren can handle it. This past year Darren has acquired a taste for beer.

The cool thing is to drink fast, get a buzz on, get high. At Dartmouth the fraternities are practically puke parties. But not just guys. You heard all sorts of wild stories about girls getting drunk and hooking up with guys they'd only just met. . . .

Darren is being jostled in this crowd; nobody knows him. He's invisible. A high school kid crushed to see ninety percent of Jill's guests are older, college age and some of them in their mid-twenties. Darren isn't usually at ease at parties, but still, he's accustomed to being known, at least. Girls from NFH zoom in on him, like fluttery little moths to the light. But here most of the girls don't even see him. Some of them look familiar, Jill's classmates from North Falls, but others are total strangers. He's wondering why Jill invited him. Why he wanted to come.

Worse yet, Darren has sighted at the edge of the noisy party some of the guys from school, as out of place in this setting as he is. Kevin Pyne, Roger Polidari, Barry Phelps and, glowering and dark-browed like some kind of beetle, Drake Hardin. Why'd Jill invite these guys!

Darren feels a stab of disgust. It's like Jill has made a fool of him.

Ross heads for his friends, eager to see them. Darren hangs back. Feeling hurt, sullen. Lifts a bottle of Coors to his mouth. He's thinking he will leave the party in a few minutes; he hates parties, anyway. At the Pynes' ski lodge in the White Mountains he and Kevin got drunk one night when Kevin's parents were out; Darren had puked his guts out in a toilet.

And in Woodstock, at parties given by people he hadn't known, he'd gotten almost as drunk. Some craziness got into him, a feeling loud and goofy— dangerous like a balloon being blown up bigger and bigger to the brink of bursting. What scared him was, at the time he wasn't scared. Once he had a few drinks, nothing could scare him.

Better hike home. It's only about two miles. Two miles is nothing for an athlete in good condition. Since the thing with Mr. Tracy, he's happiest alone anyway.

That's how Darren thinks of it. *The thing with Mr. Tracy*. Can't bring himself to think in other terms— for instance, *Mr. Tracy's death*.

His old friends, guys on the team: It's like they're contaminated somehow. Infected. Even Jimmy Kovaks he actually likes. And Mikey Eimer he has lunch with sometimes. Polidari is always trying to be friendly, and Phelps is OK; Darren knows they feel sorry about Tracy and guilty about what happened, even if they aren't about to tell anyone. But Kevin

Pyne keeps his distance, and for sure, that psycho Drake Hardin.

The Hardins live on Route 11, a half mile from the Flynns. Mrs. Hardin is a friendly acquaintance of Darren's mother. The other day returning from a trip to Wal-Mart, Darren's mother was going to drop by the Hardins' for just a minute, and Darren protested hey, no, he needed to go home.

"But it's only a minute, Darren. You can come in with me. Say hello to Priscilla, and maybe Drake will be around. You used to be friends with Drake, remember? You and him were always bicycling somewhere. What happened?"

Darren shuddered. His mother was remembering it all wrong; he'd never been friends with Drake Hardin. Not actually. Maybe when they were ten, eleven. Maybe in junior high for a while. But not for a long time.

What happened is Drake Hardin is a psycho, Mom.

What happened is I hate Drake Hardin's guts.

At school Darren just avoided them. Kevin knew to keep his distance. Darren had a new circle of friends now, a larger and looser circle of mostly Molly Rawlings's friends. The sub who'd taken Mr. Tracy's place turned out to be a really cool teacher everyone in the class liked; she was Drama Club adviser, as Mr. Tracy had been, and helped with the yearbook. Darren had gone to a few meetings of the Drama Club with Molly. Since the thing with Mr. Tracy, he'd been thinking maybe he could write a play, or a song; he'd always wanted to take guitar lessons and sing his own songs he'd written. . . . But much of the time at school he was alone. It was a surprise to realize how much work you could get done, how well you could concentrate, when you didn't waste time hanging out with your buddies, wisecracking and bullshitting. Darren spent time in the library and in chemistry lab. After school, Mr. Labrador was friendlier than in class, really nice about helping students like Darren who had trouble. Actually chemistry made sense. It was predictable. If you took it slow, you could figure it out. The last test Mr. Labrador gave, Darren's score was 82.

Still, Darren hasn't yet found out if the soul is something more than biochemistry. He seems to know if he asks Mr. Labrador, the teacher will laugh again or look serious and vague and change the subject.

Two girls are talking to Darren now. They seem amused by him: A local high school boy? A *junior*? The girls are Chi Omega "sisters" of Jill's from Durham, asking Darren where he thinks he'll be going to college. There's so much noise in the room, Darren has to raise his voice, saying deadpan his dad went to Harvard, probably he'll have to go to Harvard too, but he really, really wants to go to Durham with his friends and pledge Deke and hang out for four years. The girls lean toward Darren, impressed. One of them says approvingly, "Deke is cool," and the other says, beery and emphatic in Darren's ear, "Deke is cool."

Darren looks for a bathroom. He's jostled by

strangers, but the back of his skull has this warm buzz; he's in a mellow mood. From time to time he sees Jill Brockmeier amid the crowd, ash-blond head bobbing and weaving, scratchy voice lifted in excitement, but Jill never sees him. He wonders where her parents are: Out for the evening? Away for the weekend? The house at 82 Holland Drive is spectacular by North Falls standards. Like nothing on Route 11, for sure. It's a split-level, what looks like raw rock and plenty of glass and stucco and some kind of classy gleaming metal sprawling out on a big lot, and overlooking the country club grounds. Darren knows that his mother would be fascinated to see the Brockmeier house on the inside: the long, low leather sofas, the brick-floored vestibule, fireplaces that appear suspended in midair and numerous chrome-edged mirrors, hand-woven rugs and pots of Easter lilies. Inside the cherry-red tiled bathroom Darren has managed to locate at the rear of the house, there's an Easter lily plant in a porcelain pot so perfect-looking, you'd think it was wax except for its fragrance.

(Somebody has stubbed a cigarette out in the pot. Darren flicks the butt into the toilet.)

The bathroom is glitzy and expensive-looking but pretty messed up. Toilet seat splattered with piss. And on the tile floor a puddle.

Darren is washing his hands and regarding himself glumly in the mirror above the sink when he hears muffled voices and laughter outside the door. And a sudden loud knock, a guy's voice: "Open up! Vice squad!"

Angry, Darren unlocks and opens the door. He knows it's Kevin Pyne, grinning and defiant. And Drake Hardin crouching in a clumsy fighting posture.

Kevin's voice is slurred; his breath smells of beer. "Just checking, Flynn! Who's in here with you?" and Drake chimes in childishly, "Thought it'd be a guy, sucking Flynn off," and Kevin says, "Who sucking who off? Flynn would be sucking him off." Darren shoves past the two, disgusted. Adrenaline floods his veins; his heart is pumping for a fight. He means to walk away from the two taunting guys, but Kevin grabs his wrist, sneering, "You were seen, Flynn! In that fag's car! Your fag boyfriend Tracy, who offed himself!"

Darren can't believe what he hears. They know! Everyone must know! Still, he wants to avoid a fight. He's frightened of how angry he is, how much he wants to hit, hurt, kill. He can't let himself go; in this confused moment it's his mother Darren thinks of: how ashamed Edith Flynn would be if he got into trouble tonight. In this house.

Darren tries to make his way back to the party. He throws off Kevin's hot, gripping hand on his shoulder. Kevin says, panting, "Better not turn your back on me, Flynn! Better not dis me!" and Darren says, "Get away, you're not my friend. After what you did to Mr. Tracy," and Kevin says defiantly, "How the hell do you know what I did? You don't know, Flynn! Nobody knows, it's *con-fi-den-tial*."

Following this, things become more confused.

Mixed in with the deafening music. Raised voices

and laughter like glass shattering.

Darren tries to push Kevin away, shoving at his stocky chest with an opened palm, but Kevin shoves back. There's Drake taunting like a demented child: "Hey, Flynn! Fag Flynn! Pretty-boy Flynn kiss-kiss!" Suddenly Kevin begins the attack, grabbing Darren by his hair at the back of his head; Darren winces with pain, turns clumsily and strikes Kevin a quick hard right-hand punch to the solar plexis, a heart-stopper if properly thrown, but Darren doesn't have the momentum for such a punch, or the boxing skill, yet it's so swift and unexpected an attack that Kevin nearly goes down, with a look of astonishment. Drake is grunting and grabbing at Darren, trying to get him in a headlock. By this time the struggle is spilling into the party; girls have begun to scream. Drake leaps on Darren's back, Darren manages to turn and knee him in the groin; Kevin is pounding at Darren, red-faced and cursing; there's a sound of shattering glass; Darren scrambles against a black-lacquered table in a hallway—its sharp corner will leave a hooklike bruise in his thigh for days. People are trying to separate them by now. Drake fights and is made to sit down hard on his ass. Darren is still on his feet but light-headed, dripping blood from somewhere in his face.

Blond, neon-eyed Jill Brockmeier rushes at them, furious. Slapping at Kevin and kicking at Drake. She empties a bottle of beer onto Drake's head, where his stiff hair bristles like a porcupine's quills. "Get away! Get out of here! Both of you!" To Drake she says, with a look of savage contempt, "I didn't invite *you*, I don't even know *you*. Get out of my house before I call the police. Fat, ugly toad!" Darren is being helped to his feet. Someone has him beneath both arms. Some older guy Darren has never seen before: "'S OK, dude. Fight's all over." Darren wants to protest he doesn't need help, but he can't seem to get his breath; the adrenaline rush has left his heart still pounding. Jill leads them into a quiet room away from the party, where she switches on a desk lamp. "Put him here. Sit here, Darren. You're safe here."

Darren wants to protest to Jill he's fine, he certainly doesn't need to be protected from those assholes, but Jill is incensed, stooping over him to examine his face. There's a box of Kleenex on a shelf; she grabs wads of tissue and swipes at the blood. "Those crude bastards. Those *punks*. I can't believe this happened *at my party*."

Next Darren knows, he's alone in the room. Jill has left him with the box of Kleenex. The booming music seems to flood back. Also there are raised voices, what sounds like doors slamming. Darren's right eye is beginning to swell, and his mouth. The blood is coming from his mouth, he thinks. And there's a quickening pain inside his head. As the adrenaline rush subsides, he'll feel like shit. He knows, the sensation is bad enough after just a swim meet, where there's no physical contact, no exchange of blows and (in theory) no actual pain.

Never run, never cry.

Fast and furious.

He'll feel like shit, but at least he knows if Walt

Flynn had witnessed the fight, he wouldn't have been ashamed of his son.

And he has to laugh, Jill Brockmeier pouring beer on Drake Hardin's head. Funny! The way Jill called him a fat, ugly toad. Everyone at North Falls High will be talking and laughing over this for a long time. "Fat ugly toad," even nice girls like Molly Rawlings won't be able to resist whispering and laughing when Drake Hardin passes by in the hall.

Darren's mouth hurts; he can't help laughing.

Darren continues to press wads of tissue against his face. Jill should have taken him to a bathroom, not somebody's study. He sees that he has dripped blood onto a desk. Not an ordinary desk like some teacher's desk at school but an oval slab of polished wood, the beautiful burnished color of horse chestnuts. This blood he can wipe away with tissues, but he's dripped more blood onto papers with the letterhead of a pharmaceutical company. There are columns of figures beneath such mysterious categories as "Shares Outstanding," "Float," "Recent Price," "Year

Low/Year High." On the desk is a state-of-the-art computer like no computer Darren has ever seen before, so sleek. Must be he's in Mr. Brockmeier's home office. He should alert Jill that he has dripped blood onto her father's financial papers. But maybe he won't see Jill again. He's about ready to go home, and he isn't about to return to the family room to find her.

Except: His head is so heavy! His eyelids keep closing. He is hoping that at home his parents will be in bed by the time he gets back. Dad could handle Darren looking beat up, but not Mom. You have to shield your mom from so much, but it's worth it.

Tomorrow, well—he'll worry about tomorrow. Can't worry about tomorrow before it arrives, right?

"Darren? Oh, God, are you *alive*?"

Jill Brockmeier is tugging at him, distraught. Darren is startled, lifting his heavy head from the desk. Can't believe he's been sleeping!—or whatever state his head has been in, stuporous as a coma.

(What time is it? Darren wonders. His watch seems to be broken. High-decibel music is still booming from another part of the house, but everything feels later.)

Jill tugs at Darren, urging him to his feet. She seems to be in a mild panic, as if she's forgotten him until now. She exudes an air of perfumy urgency, girl sweat and beer. Her flimsy see-through top is damp from perspiration. Jill apologizes to Darren, calling him sweetie, honey. Almost, you'd believe she's sincere. She is walking him up a flight of stairs, slowly. Darren wants to go home, Darren is sure he's fine by now, the bleeding has stopped, he's rested and OK, but Jill is adamant, he needs first aid. She has slipped an arm around his waist so that he can't lose his balance or break away from her. For such a thin frantic girl Jill is surprisingly strong. And her will is stronger.

"First aid, sweetie. Can't let you go home looking like a plane crash."

Jill is swaying on her (bare) feet. She's several

inches shorter than Darren, so you'd almost mistake her for younger than Darren, but Darren knows better. Jill Brockmeier is a lot older than he is.

In a bathroom of sparkling coral tile and floor-to-ceiling panel mirrors, Jill sits Darren on a cushioned stool in front of the sink so that she can rinse his swollen and bloody face, tenderly. "Oh, God! Your eye. Your mouth. And you're so handsome, Darren. So sexy. It's kind of ridiculous." Jill laughs her throaty, hoarse laugh. Jill shudders. "I hope your father won't sue my father, Darren. Promise me you won't tell where this happened?" Darren laughs and says sure, he promises. "But I'm serious, Darren. My dad would kill me if he knew those guys were here, beating up on one of my guests." Darren says his dad isn't the type to sue, he doesn't trust lawyers. Jill says that her dad is a lawyer, in fact, but Darren has the right idea, never trust a lawyer. "Never trust anybody if you can help it. Promise, Darren! You're so *young*." Darren can't see the logic here, but he's laughing, he guesses this is funny. Face throbbing with pain, but still, this is funny. Shyly he glances at himself in a mirror and is horrified at how he looks, the bruised, swollen eye and his mouth like pounded meat and his nostrils leaking blood.

Yet Jill Brockmeier, whom he scarcely knows, is calling him handsome, sexy.

Makes no sense! None of it.

He's shocked, too, to see how bloodstained his clothes are. The expensive blue woolen sweater Molly Rawlings gave him for Christmas he has hardly worn. He'll have to shield from her the sight of the beautiful sweater so stained and clotted with blood it can never be made clean again.

Jill rinses Darren's numerous facial wounds, dabs them with a stinging liquid and neatly affixes Band-Aids. Some of these are clunky white squares. Jill even tries to wrap gauze around Darren's head, but the effect is too comical. She soaks a cloth in cold water and holds it against his nose, which won't stop bleeding; she urges him to tip his head back. Holds him in a kind of headlook, as his mother might have done. Darren wants to squirm free but acquiesces. Jill is so adamant, it's easier to give in. Nothing like Molly Rawlings, or any other girl Darren has known well. He admires the chic short-cropped blond hair; in the bright overhead lights he can see dark-brown roots. And there's the flimsy glitter top slipping off one of Jill's shoulders; Darren can make out the girl's fist-sized hard-looking breasts, berry-size nipples and the suggestion of her collarbone beneath her creamy-pale skin. Jill's nakedness seems a kind of unconsciousness; Darren feels both protective of her and aroused.

Darren wants to go home. Darren is anxious, excited. A hot rush of blood to his groin, he's miserable suddenly. Jill protests in a hurt voice, "You don't want to go home yet, Darren. Your nose is so tender." She kisses him, lightly at first. Darren grabs her around the hips, and Jill staggers above him, laughing. Darren is so excited, he has begun to tremble. The throbbing in his head has vanished; all the blood in his head is rushing downward. Jill runs her hands over him, teasing. She has him on his feet, leading him stumbling and half blinded into her bedroom, must be her bedroom; Darren is short of breath clutching at Jill, trying to catch her elusive pouty mouth with his own. He has a confused impression of glossy wall posters—Grand Canyon, Grand Tetons, Yosemite, Joshua Tree Monument. The room is several times larger than his own room. There are clothes scattered everywhere underfoot. There's a smell of powder, cosmetics. A bed with a canopy and on it enormous patchwork pillows and, Darren is touched to see, Raggedy Ann dolls.

These dolls Jill unceremoniously tosses. The big pillows go flying. For the second time within a couple of hours Darren feels as if he is spinning out of control. His life is being snatched from him, flung away somewhere unknown to be returned to him dazed and numbed and astonishing.

Like finishing first in the four-hundred-meter freestyle. Way beyond brain chemistry. It's like his

soul has gone up in a sheet of flame. He collapses on
the sweaty, squirmy, laughing blond girl half sobbing
in gratitude.

". . . this guy I see a lot, at Durham, he isn't here
tonight, we're in some kind of 'transitional' stage and
I'm, like, thinking it's a 'terminal' stage, and what
about you, Darren Flynn, I suppose you have a girlfriend . . ."

Jill is curled up against Darren in a little-girl posture of vulnerability, both her slender legs bent and
one arm flung across Darren's chest, so he's uneasily
aware of the blue-glaring fingernails a few inches
from his face. Darren is lying on his back in this unfamiliar marshmallow-soft bed feeling as if he has fall-
en from a great height and is lying now stunned,
unmoving.

". . . or girlfriends. Lots of girlfriends. It's OK,
you can tell me, Darren. I won't be hurt."

Darren doesn't know how to answer. He senses
that he's being interrogated. Says no, he doesn't have

a girlfriend, he has a close friend who is a girl.

Jill wants to know her name. Darren says that's private.

Jill says, stung, "Don't tell her my name then."

Darren is thinking that Molly Rawlings is the only girl he really likes and respects, and she's too good for him. She's too serious for him. Having sex with Molly the way he has had sex with Jill Brockmeier isn't possible; he would only hurt Molly, and he can't risk that.

Jill changes the subject, asking Darren about summer: Will he be in North Falls?

"No. I'm going away for the summer."

"Where?"

"My uncle's place, in Maine."

"Where in Maine?"

Darren hesitates. He's uncomfortable being questioned like this. He's beginning to see how a girl like Jill could eat you alive like what's that insect: praying mantis. The female of the species devours the male after they mate!

"North of Portland. A farm."

"A farm? In *Maine?*"

Jill considers this as she'd consider some really far-out possibility, sardine yogurt, for instance, the normal-girl reaction is to grimace in disdain, but Jill is trying to see how, if really hot Darren Flynn is going to spend summer on a farm in Maine, it has got to be a possibility.

Until this moment Darren hasn't thought much about the summer. Except in a general way vague with apprehension and dread, how would he avoid the guys, how would he avoid vultures eager to bring up the topic of Mr. Tracy, the disgust and anger he'd feel for people getting off on somebody else's misery, and summer would trap him in North Falls in his usual routine . . . Except suddenly it comes to him: He'll go to stay with his aunt Midge and his uncle Harvey on their farm at Spruce Head on the coast, seventy miles north of Portland. When he and Eddy were younger, they spent a lot of time there. They loved their Spruce Head summers, helping with farmwork; it wasn't easy work and they didn't get paid, but Darren especially loved Spruce Head and didn't understand why those summers stopped a couple of years ago. Darren's uncle Harvey is his favorite relative; he's lot more mellow than his older brother, Walt. He raises dairy cows, grows potatoes and corn in the short Maine season. He has a twelve-foot outboard motorboat he takes out onto the choppy Atlantic, fishing for bluefish and striped bass. Every time he calls Walt, Harvey asks to speak to Darren, teases him asking how the guitar is, if he's had time for lessons?

". . . this really cool place in Boothbay Harbor, these friends of my dad's. It's, like, a resort hotel it's so big, and he's got a forty-foot yacht, and two sailboats." Jill is speaking animatedly, leaning on an elbow above Darren, who hasn't been listening closely to her, he's excited thinking he will ask his uncle to give him guitar lessons again, the two of them can play together. Darren is thinking he wants to learn to play guitar more than anything in the world, he wants to compose his own songs.

He has so much to express!

Jill sees his attention has drifted from her. She nudges him in the ribs with a hard little jab. The glisten of her skin reminds Darren of fine-ground mica. She asks, "Maybe I could come visit you, Darren? If I'm in Boothbay?"

Darren's eye is swelling shut; he has a vague worry maybe his nose is cracked. But he's the happiest he has been in a long time.

Darren laughs. "Sure."

JOYCE CAROL OATES is the renowned author of many novels. *Big Mouth & Ugly Girl* was a finalist for the *Los Angeles Times* Book Prize, and *Freaky Green Eyes* was named a *Publishers Weekly* Best Book. A recipient of the National Book Award and the PEN/Malamud Award for Excellence in Short Fiction, Ms. Oates is the Roger S. Berlind Distinguished Professor of the Humanities at Princeton University. In 2003 she was a recipient of the Common Wealth Award for Distinguished Service in Literature. She lives in Princeton, New Jersey.